"Everything's Going To Be All Right,"

Tuck said, stroking her hair.

"Hold me, Tuck. Please hold me," Nicole whispered.

He turned slightly to bring her closer, and when he did, her hands slid up his chest to the back of his neck. She pressed tightly against him.

His heart started hammering. He'd only intended to offer comfort, but their embrace was becoming sexual. Even knowing he should stop it here and now, he didn't. The woman in his arms felt like no other he'd ever held. Her scent was unique, as was the texture of her hair and skin.

She lifted her chin to look at him, and he saw the glaze of emotions gone wild in her beautiful blue eyes. In the back of his mind was a suspicion that she was not fully aware of what she was doing. But her upturned lips and beseeching expression couldn't be ignored. Nor could he be so cruel as to turn his back on her when she needed him most.

If that need had evolved into desire, so be it.

Dear Reader,

We all know that Valentine's Day is the most romantic holiday of the year. It's the day you show that special someone in your life—husband, fiancé…even your mom!—just how much you care by giving them special gifts of love.

And our special Valentine's gift to you is a book from a writer many of you have said is one of your favorites, Annette Broadrick. *Megan's Marriage* isn't just February's MAN OF THE MONTH, it's also the first book of Annette's brand-new DAUGHTERS OF TEXAS series. This passionate love story is just right for Valentine's Day.

February also marks the continuation of SONS AND LOVERS, a bold miniseries about three men who discover that love and family are the most important things in life. In *Reese: The Untamed* by Susan Connell, a dashing bachelor meets his match and begins to think that being married might be more pleasurable than he'd ever dreamed. The series continues in March with *Ridge: The Avenger* by Leanne Banks.

This month is completed with four more scintillating love stories: *Assignment: Marriage* by Jackie Merritt, *Daddy's Choice* by Doreen Owens Malek, *This Is My Child* by Lucy Gordon and *Husband Material* by Rita Rainville. Don't miss any of them!

So Happy Valentine's Day and Happy Reading!

Lucia Macro
Senior Editor

Please address questions and book requests to:
Silhouette Reader Service
U.S.: 3010 Walden Ave., P.O. Box 1325, Buffalo, NY 14269
Canadian: P.O. Box 609, Fort Erie, Ont. L2A 5X3

JACKIE MERRITT
ASSIGNMENT: MARRIAGE

SILHOUETTE *Desire*®
Published by Silhouette Books
America's Publisher of Contemporary Romance

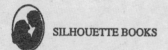

SILHOUETTE BOOKS

ISBN 0-373-05980-9

ASSIGNMENT: MARRIAGE

Copyright © 1996 by C.J. Books, Inc.

Printed in U.S.A.

JACKIE MERRITT

and her husband live just outside of Las Vegas, Nevada. An accountant for many years, Jackie has happily traded numbers for words. Next to family, books are her greatest joy. She started writing in 1987 and her efforts paid off in 1988 with the publication of her first novel. When she's not writing or enjoying a good book, Jackie dabbles in watercolor painting and likes playing the piano in her spare time.

Prologue

The streets were close to empty. Even in Las Vegas most people were home in bed at three in the morning. Of course, if night owls wanted action, they could find it in Vegas at any hour.

Sergeant Tuck Hannigan, who had eleven years under his belt with the Metropolitan Police Department, was finally ready to call it a day. It had been a hell of a fifteen-hour stretch for him. Normal shifts ran ten hours, but there were some that never seemed to end.

Tuck made a right turn and spotted an around-the-clock convenience store. Remembering that he'd used the last grounds in the coffee can in his kitchen about eighteen hours ago, he pulled into the store's brightly lighted parking lot. One other car occupied a space, a battered old blue sedan. Tuck parked beside it.

He was wearing civvies—jeans, a black T-shirt, a light-weight jacket and sneakers. His present duty required the standard police officer's uniform, but he'd changed at the station before leaving. He was beat, getting a little bleary-eyed, but he knew he'd want coffee when he got up in the morning.

Switching off the ignition, he swung out of the car and started for the convenience store's front door. Only a few steps from his car he realized that he couldn't see anyone inside. The building was almost garish with lights. There were windows all along the front of it, and inside there wasn't a person in sight.

Tuck glanced back to the old sedan and felt a spurt of adrenaline. Something was wrong. Convenience stores were notorious targets for robberies and this setup looked suspicious. He eased back toward his car and then ducked around it, intending to go to the pay phone at the side of the building. In two minutes he could run the sedan's license plate and receive information on its owner.

All hell suddenly broke loose. The sharp pop of gunshots and a woman's scream came from within the store. Tuck drew the weapon from the holster in the small of his back and raced for the entrance of the store. He hit the swinging door at a dead run. Two men burst from the back room, guns blazing. Tuck threw himself on the floor and fired at the same time. The men went down.

It was over in seconds. Tuck's heart felt like it was trying to bust through the wall of his chest. He lay there, breathing hard, sweating. A woman teetered from the back room, holding her hand to her left shoulder, which was wet with blood.

Tuck struggled to his feet. The woman looked dazed. "You shot them," she said in a hoarse, cracking voice.

He looked at the men on the floor, went over to them and checked each for a pulse. They were young, probably under twenty. One was bearded, one's head was shaved. He sensed the woman sinking and rushed to help her. He sat her on a box and went to the phone and dialed a number.

*

"This is Sergeant Tuck Hannigan. Send an ambulance to..." He recited the particulars. "There are two dead and one injured. I killed two men."

He put the phone down and realized there was blood on the front of his clothes. He looked down at it and felt the onslaught of pain. He'd been hit.

The glaring lights in the store began to blur. He sank to the floor. The last thing he remembered was the wail of sirens and the sight of the two young men, dead, lying in their own blood next to a candy display.

One

The convenience store shootings made the headlines. Tuck was questioned until he was sick of telling the story. For three days he'd been unaware of the hoopla as he'd been in and out of consciousness in the Intensive Care Unit of Las Vegas's Humana Hospital. But the day he was moved to the surgical recovery wing, the questions started.

Then there was the hearing. Anytime a police officer was involved in a shooting, he was put on suspension and a hearing was held so the community could assess the situation. Tuck was completely exonerated of any wrongdoing or errors in judgment. The case was clear: he had fired his weapon to protect himself and the female clerk, who'd obviously already been injured.

He had made no mistakes. Everyone told him so and he knew it himself. But it was the first time he'd had to use his service revolver against another human being, and two men had died. Two very young men.

Never mind that they had a record a mile long. Never

mind that they had shot the thirty-two-year-old clerk, who had three children, a husband and a mother and father who loved and needed her. The woman was all right, thank God. She, too, had had to endure a stay in the hospital, and physically she was recovering. But she would probably never feel safe again. Tuck worked with victims organizations on occasion, and most people had a hard time getting over the trauma of physical and mental maltreatment.

Regardless that the woman was going to make it and Tuck wasn't blamed for the shootings, he couldn't get past the horrifying incident. He had killed two people, two men who weren't even old enough to vote.

As was strict policy, he had to attend scheduled sessions with one of the department's psychologists, a Laura Keaton.

Laura was a levelheaded woman, around forty-five, Tuck estimated. He liked her voice, which was low and pleasantly modulated. She talked common sense, too, none of that medical gibberish that he only just barely understood.

This was his second visit to Dr. Keaton's office. The first had been brief; a handshake, over which she had told him to call her "Laura" and a low-key discussion of departmental routines that had put Tuck at ease.

Today was going to be different he realized when Laura said, "You were married once, Tuck. What happened?"

They were seated on comfortable furniture in a corner of her office, he on the sofa, Laura on a chair. Her brown eyes behind stylish glasses reflected nothing other than a professional interest, both in her question and whatever answer he might give her.

But he couldn't see what his failed marriage had to do with the present situation. "That was a long time ago, Doc."

"How long?"

He withheld a rising impatience. "I was twenty-three when I got married. It lasted three years. I'm now thirty-four."

Laura tented her fingers and regarded the ruggedly handsome man sitting so rigidly before her. Thick dark hair. Somber gray eyes. "You were married the year you joined the force?"

She had her dates down pat. "Yes."

Laura consulted the folder on her lap. "No children?"

The muscles in Tuck's jaw clenched. "There was one, a boy. He died at three months of age."

Laura raised her eyes and drew a slow breath. "I'm sorry. Tell me about it, Tuck."

He looked away, letting his gaze drift to three filled bookcases, to a painting on the wall that depicted a harbor and a fleet of fishing boats, and finally to her desk. A framed photograph caught his attention. It was of Laura, a smiling, dark-haired man and two teenage boys; her family, obviously.

His eyes returned to Dr. Keaton. "May I smoke?"

She smiled. "I'm not going to lecture you on how bad smoking is for your cardiovascular system, Tuck. Smoke if you'd like."

"Thanks." He grinned slightly. "For permission and for not lecturing."

Laura got up for an ashtray she kept in a desk drawer. She had long ago realized that some people couldn't speak at all without smoking, and a nervous, incoherent patient was a waste of her time and his. "Are you a heavy smoker?" She sat down again.

"At times."

"Lately?"

Tuck inhaled the first puff from his cigarette. "Yeah." He blew out the smoke. "Timmy...that was his name...died of pneumonia. That's what the doctors said, anyway. What he really died from was neglect." Tuck looked at the tip of his cigarette intently. "Jeanie, my wife, wasn't much of a mother. I was still relatively new to the department, working crazy hours, taking on any extra duty I could nail down. I didn't even know he was sick. I went to work one day...he seemed fine . . . and they called me from the hospital before my shift was over. He died the next day.''

"It must have been a particularly virulent strain of pneumonia, Tuck," Laura said softly.

"So they said, and the antibiotics they gave him made him go into convulsions. There wasn't anything they could do."

"But you blamed your wife."

Tuck's hard eyes met hers. "I still do. She left him that day with a thirteen-year-old girl from the neighborhood. She knew he was sick and she left him with a kid. At least the girl was smart enough to know she had a sick baby on her hands, 'cause she called 9-1-1. I finally found Jeanie that night in a bar, half drunk and giggling with some joker she'd picked up."

"And that was the end of your marriage."

Tuck grinned cynically. "Not a pretty story, is it?"

"I've heard worse. What about family? Parents? Brothers and sisters?"

"My dad died when I was fifteen. My mother lives in Phoenix. She came while I was in the hospital, but she's not very well. No brothers. One sister, who lives back east. We talk on the phone once in a while."

"Friends? Let me rephrase that. Do you have friends outside of the department?"

"A few."

"Anyone important?"

"If you're fishing to find out if there's a woman in my life, Doc, it's been a long, dry spell."

"Never been tempted to remarry?"

"Never," Tuck replied emphatically.

Laura paused, then smiled. "You're beginning to look fit, but how are you feeling physically?"

"The wounds are healing." He'd taken two bullets, one in the chest, one in the right thigh.

"Can we talk about that night?"

Tuck snuffed out his cigarette in the ashtray. "You're the doctor. What do you want to know?"

"How you felt during the incident."

Tuck laughed shortly. "I didn't have time to feel anything."

"All right, after it was over then. You were lucid enough to phone in and report what had happened. What were you feeling?"

"Sick."

"In pain?"

"Not at first. All I could see were those two bodies on the floor."

"Did you feel justified in shooting those men?"

"Justified? No, that never entered my mind."

"What did? Think about it, Tuck. What did enter your mind?"

He swallowed the rising gorge in his throat, and when he spoke, his voice cracked. "I . . . don't remember."

Nicole Currie couldn't sit still. The two men in her living room wore dark suits and expressions almost as dark. Nicole stopped pacing and threw up her hands. "How can you ask me to do such a thing? I have a life, a job, this house, friends. I can't just disappear!"

John Harper and Scott Paulsen, both police officers, exchanged glances. John, who was the older by a good fifteen years, stood. "You can't stay here, Nicole." He'd spent enough time in Nicole's company during the past four days to call her by her first name. "The prosecuting attorney needs time to prepare a solid case against Lowicki and Spencer. You're our only witness."

"I wouldn't be your witness if I'd thought it through before reporting what I saw," Nicole said sharply. It had seemed so cut-and-dried at the time. Two men leaving a building and getting into a car, a simple act. But the next morning she'd read in the paper about the double murder in that building, in apartment 17A. She'd gotten a good look at the men, particularly the one with the jagged scar that crimped his left cheek. The murders, the newspaper article recited, quoting Detective John Harper, had taken place at approximately 1:00 a.m. *Any person with information regarding this crime should contact Detective Harper at Metro headquarters.*

It was all by accident, of course. Normally, Nicole wasn't even in that part of town, and certainly not at the ungodly hour of 1:00 a.m. But she'd attended a bridal shower for a co-worker. Nicole was the purchasing agent for the Monte Carlo Hotel and Casino, a massive operation that kept her and three assistants on their toes. On her way home from the shower, which had turned out to be a gala affair and had lasted much longer than anticipated, her car had acted up. With the motor coughing and sputtering, she had managed to pull it to the curb.

Then she'd sat there and looked at the dark street and felt fear developing. Hers was the only car on the block. To her right was vacant land, black as ink and all but invisible. The nearest streetlight was some distance away, the nearest lighted building even farther. She'd forced herself out of the car and down the sidewalk toward the building. It was an apartment house, she realized, a rather nice one, which made her feel better.

She was in the shadow of an immense bank of oleander bushes when two men came walking out the front door. It was herself she was thinking of when she sank deeper into the shadows. It simply wasn't smart for a woman alone to show herself to two strange men at one in the morning.

They didn't see her, she was positive. They walked to the car at the curb, a black or dark blue Lincoln with Nevada plates, got in and drove away. The only thing that gave her pause was the way the Lincoln had slowed as it passed her red Toyota.

It was the one factor that made her think that just possibly the police weren't being too conscientious about her protection.

But disappear? They were suggesting some sort of witness protection plan, leaving Las Vegas, using an assumed name, telling no one—*no one*—what she was doing. What about her job? Couldn't she at least tell her employers?

"We can't risk telling anyone, Nicole," John Harper said solemnly. "Not at this point. Call your employer with a story of a family emergency. Tell them you have to leave immediately and will be in touch. We'd like you to pack and be ready to leave by tonight. Scott will stay here in the house with you until then."

Nicole tossed her head back, as though to twitch long hair away from her face. Her nearly black hair *had* been long until a week ago when she'd gone to her favorite hairdresser for a cut and new style.

"I could be fired," she said despondently. "It's taken me years to work up to my present position."

"A job's not as valuable as your life," Scott said quietly.

"Nicole," John said, "the minute it's safe to do so, I'll talk to your employers myself."

"But you said it could take months. The Monte Carlo cannot function without a purchasing agent for months." Nicole was sick about this and couldn't pretend otherwise.

The older man sighed. "I know it can't."

Nicole felt a shiver go up her spine. There were other aspects of the situation that scared her witless. "I'll be completely alone in a strange place. You two might not understand this, but the idea of living where I won't know a soul is terrifying. I was born and raised in Las Vegas. I've never lived anywhere else."

"You won't be alone," John said softly.

Nicole's left eyebrow shot up. "I won't? Who would be going with me?"

"We're working that out, but he'll be a police officer."

"He? Why not a woman?"

"It might be a woman. Nothing's set yet. Don't worry. Whoever picks you up tonight will be well qualified to protect you."

Rubbing her arms as though chilled, Nicole went to look out the window. "This is a nightmare."

John was instantly at her side and pulling her back. "Please. Don't go near the windows."

Nicole gave up. Her legs were weak, her stomach churning. The thought of leaving everything familiar was horrible. It wasn't fair that only doing what she'd felt was any citizen's duty should result in this. But if she took a stand and refused, what then? The men she'd seen had, according to the police, already killed two people. Would killing one more bother them? Especially if that person's testimony could convict them of murder?

"I'll be ready tonight," she said numbly. "Can you tell me where I'll be going?"

John shook his head with a sympathetic smile. "Sorry. I don't know that myself."

"Well, Tuck," Captain Joe Crawford said when Tuck walked into his office. "How're you doing? Sit down. Make yourself comfortable."

"Thanks." Tuck took a seat.

"Feeling all right?"

"Not bad. I got a call to come in and see you." When Tuck had started out with the department, Joe Crawford had been his sergeant. They had eleven years of common ground and a good, solid relationship. "What's going on, Joe?"

"Your suspension's been lifted."

Tuck nodded. "That's good." It was a lie. He wasn't ready to go back to work and wasn't sure if he ever would be. "Joe, I've been thinking about taking my accumulated vacation time and sick leave. It adds up to about six weeks."

Joe regarded him across the wide desk between them. "Need a little more time off, eh? Well, that's not a bad idea, Tuck. You had a rough go of it. Went through it myself once."

"Yeah, I know." Tuck leaned forward. "Joe, how long was it before you got over it?"

Joe sucked in a long, thoughtful breath. "Not sure I ever did. But it does get easier, Tuck."

Tuck hoped so. He wasn't sleeping well, or eating much. Those were a couple of facts he'd neglected to mention to Dr. Keaton.

There was a lengthy silence. Tuck lit a cigarette. "Is it okay, then, to use my vacation and sick time?"

"Sure, no problem. By the way, if all you want to do is get out of town for a while, there's a real cushy job available."

"What is it?"

"Protecting the witness who can place Nick Lowicki at the exact site of the Buckley murders."

Tuck's eyes narrowed. "There's a witness?"

"A reliable one. An upstanding citizen, Tuck, clean as a whistle."

"Does Lowicki know?"

"We're not sure. He didn't do it alone, Tuck. We think the other man the witness saw was Gil Spencer. Anyway, the witness's car was parked on the street in plain sight, and Spencer and Lowicki might be lowlifes, but they're not completely stupid."

Tuck turned his head and laughed sardonically. "Thought you mentioned a *cushy* job. Better get my hearing checked."

Joe leaned forward. "Tuck, it *will* be cushy. We're moving the witness to...well, I'll tell you that if you get involved, but I guarantee you'd like the place. Look, all you'd have to do is keep the witness company. We're really keeping the lid tight on this one. Only a few of our top people even know there is a witness, even fewer know what we're planning to do. What do you say? It would be like a vacation with pay, and you wouldn't use up your accumulated days. Afterward, if you still need more time away from the job, you can take it."

"Why me?"

Joe cleared his throat while sitting back. "Because you've got a perfect excuse to disappear for an extended leave." Joe hesitated before adding, "And you're unencumbered, Tuck. There's no one at home to ask questions."

It wasn't at all what he'd thought he might do with his free time. Actually, he didn't know what he might do, but he sure hadn't thought of anything like this.

"Can I think about it, Joe?"

Joe shook his head. "There's no time. The witness will be ready to leave tonight."

Tuck butted his cigarette, got up and went to a window. He stared out and absently watched traffic. "Can you tell me anything about it?"

"Not unless you agree. No one's going to know anything unless they're involved up to their eyeballs. We're going to nail Lowicki this time, Tuck, but we don't have a positive ID on the other guy. We need time to box him in, to prove that he was with Lowicki at 1:00 a.m. that night. The prosecutor's office wants an airtight case before we haul them in. That's what we'll work on while you—or someone like you—takes care of the witness."

Tuck mulled it over. Nick Lowicki was a snake. A drug dealer, a pimp, the sort of man the law enforcement community referred to as street scum. He'd made a bad mistake and there was a witness who could positively finger him. If the D.A. could build a case and put Gil Spencer away at the same time, the streets would be just a little bit cleaner.

"Well, guess I don't have anything better to do," Tuck said quietly.

"Then you'll do it?"

Tuck turned. "I'll do it. Now, can you fill me in?"

"Tonight, Tuck. Just before you leave. Meet me back here at nine this evening. Have your things with you. I'll give you a car and some money. You'll pick up the witness and be out of town before ten."

Captain Joe Crawford didn't just hand over a car and some cash that night, he had a whole new ID prepared for Tuck, a driver's license, a social security card, and a couple of credit cards. "The credit cards are strictly for show, Tuck. Don't want you using them and leaving any kind of trail. There's enough cash here to last you for several weeks, and there'll be more available if you need it."

Tuck studied the handful of cards. "So, my name's going to be Tom King."

"Nice simple name, Tuck. That's how we're going to introduce you to the witness, as Tom King. No need for her to know your real name. She's no pro at this sort of thing and might make a slip at the wrong time."

Tuck regarded his captain. "The witness is a woman? How old is she?"

Joe Crawford cleared his throat. "I don't know, maybe thirty, thirty-one."

"She's not married?"

"No. Now, Tuck, don't get that bullheaded look on your face. What difference does it make? You'd be doing the same job if the witness was a sixty-year-old man."

"It never occurred to me we were talking about a woman, a *young* woman." Tuck shook his head disgustedly. "Tell me she's buck-toothed, stringy-haired and ugly."

Joe laughed. "Can't do that. She's a pretty woman."

"Aw, hell," Tuck muttered.

An hour later, briefed on his destination in great detail and as ready to go as he'd ever be, Tuck and John Harper got into the assigned car, with John at the wheel. Tuck hadn't asked the woman's real name. Joe had told him that her assumed name was Cheryl King, and then quickly added, "The two of you can decide what kind of arrangement you'd be most comfortable with. You could be sister and brother, if that makes you happy. Personally, I like the idea of a couple, a husband and wife."

"Dammit, Joe, you set me up!"

Joe had smiled blandly. "You'll enjoy yourself in Idaho, Tuck. Coeur d'Alene's a beautiful little city."

While John Harper drove to the woman's home, Tuck glared out the side window. If Joe Crawford had even hinted at the witness's sex and age, Tuck would have refused the job with gusto. He didn't want to spend the next month, or whatever it took, with a woman.

John pulled into a driveway. "Well, here we are, Tuck."

Tuck didn't immediately jump out. "I don't like this, Harper. I don't like it one damn bit!"

John shrugged, as if to say, *Tough, Tuck! You took the job, you live with it.* But then the older man relented and smiled. "She's a nice woman, Tuck. You'll like her."

"Like hell I will," he muttered as he got out of the car.

Inside, Nicole was back to pacing. Scott Paulsen answered the back door, and Nicole stayed in the living room. She was dressed for a long ride, wearing old jeans, faded and soft from a hundred washings, a plain, blue T-shirt and sneakers. She was pale and biting the thumbnail on her left hand, a habit she abhorred and thought she'd cured herself of more than a dozen years ago.

Scott, John, and a third man walked in. Nicole's anxious blue eyes went instantly to the stranger. John made the introductions. "Cheryl, this is Tom."

"Hello," Nicole mumbled. Tom was stiff and unsmiling. Tall, well-built, wearing jeans that rivaled her own for age and comfort. Inscrutable gray eyes.

"Hello," Tuck said tonelessly, refusing to acknowledge Cheryl's pretty face and long legs. Two large and two small suitcases sat near the sofa. "I'll get these loaded." Scott moved to help and between them they carried all four cases out to the car.

Nicole looked around her living room. Crying would do nothing beyond reddening her eyes, but she felt like busting loose with a wounded wail. Instead she began snapping off lamps. The house was already locked and as secure as it could get.

"Well . . . guess I'm ready," she said listlessly.

John Harper offered a consoling smile. "Nicole, this will all be over in no time. You'll see."

She wasn't consoled. Weeks—maybe months—away from her home and job didn't seem like "no time" to her.

John pulled an envelope out of his inside coat pocket. "Scott filled you in on destination and identity. Tom's been given most of the money, but we thought you should have some, too, just in case."

Nicole took the envelope. "In case of what, John? Tom's trustworthy, isn't he?"

"He's the best there is, Nicole. Don't worry about that. He's got eleven years with the department and has experience in every phase of law enforcement."

"Tom's not his real name."

"No."

Looking around one last time, Nicole sighed. "Come on," John said gently. "You've got a long trip ahead of you."

"One more question, John. Why are we driving to Idaho, rather than flying?"

"Everyone thought it would be best, Nicole. We're keeping your departure as low-key as possible. There's very little way of telling if some stranger follows you onto a plane, but driving north out of Vegas, the road is long and empty. Tom will know if anyone's behind you."

Nicole left several lights burning in the house, at John's suggestion. They went through the back door and Nicole locked the dead bolt. She was carrying her purse, into which she'd tucked the envelope of cash. Her suitcases were jammed with clothes of every description. No one knew how long she'd have to stay away, and that was probably the hardest part of this whole discomfiting ordeal. At John Harper's instruction she'd written a dozen cards to friends, all with the same carefully worded message. *Family emergency calls me away. Don't worry. I'll be in touch.* Hopefully the simple message would forestall someone panicking and raising a public fuss because they couldn't reach her.

Tuck was leaning against the car. He straightened as Nicole and John approached. "All set?"

"All set," John said quietly.

"Who's driving?" Nicole questioned.

"I am," Tuck said flatly.

Nicole got in the passenger side, Tuck got behind the wheel. John leaned down to peer through the open window. "Take care."

"Yeah," Tuck drawled, and started the motor.

Nicole fastened her seatbelt. The car backed out of her driveway without lights. They were two blocks away from her house before Tuck switched on the headlights. Nicole was battling tears and looking straight ahead.

Tuck took a maze of back streets to reach Highway 95. The fuel gauge indicated a full tank of gas. They wouldn't have to make a stop for hours. He glanced at the woman sitting so silently and registered her rigid profile.

Her silence was welcome. He turned his attention back to the road.

Two

Once out of Vegas the road became black and almost eerily vacant. Highway 95 was an important link between Las Vegas and Reno, but away from those two cities, Nevada's roads were sparsely traveled. Ten, fifteen minutes would pass between oncoming cars. There were none behind him, Tuck was certain. None with headlights at least.

He eyed his silent companion. "Mind if I turn on the radio?"

Nicole's head barely moved in a brief glance. "Go ahead."

Tuck turned on the power, drove with one hand and fiddled with the radio with the other, trying to pick up a station. After a few minutes he gave up. "There's nothing but static." The car was an inexpensive blue sedan, and apparently the radio was a weakly powered model.

Driving the dark road, Tuck's thoughts turned to his last session with Dr. Keaton. *I'm not going to preach to you, Tuck. You're going to have to deal with your conscience in your own way. You did nothing wrong, and that's what you must come to accept.* He had answered, *I did nothing illegal, Doc.* She had slowly nodded her understanding.

He understood, too, which relieved none of the tension in his gut. What else could he ever be but a cop? And yet he couldn't see himself back on the street and dealing with the myriad problems he'd previously faced so confidently.

This trip, this witness protection job, was eating at him. He shouldn't have let Joe talk him into it. He didn't want to protect anyone. He wasn't wearing his gun, although he had it with him, tucked under his seat on the floor of the car. Joe had described the job as "cushy," and maybe it would be. He'd been to northern Idaho once before and liked what he'd seen. Certainly it was different from southern Nevada, with lush, green-forested mountains and numerous lakes. Beautiful scenery, unquestionably. And the chance of Lowicki and Spencer tracking Cheryl so far north, once they discovered there was a witness who could unequivocally tie them to the murders, was slim to none.

But spending weeks with a woman he didn't know, nor had any desire to know, was damn disturbing. He really hadn't thought about the witness's gender when Joe first brought up the subject, assuming, obviously, that they were talking about a man.

Well, there was nothing manly about "Cheryl King." She was pure woman, every inch of her, and some exotic scent wafted his way every time she moved.

She wasn't moving very much, he had to admit. It was as though her gaze was glued to the windshield. In the dash lights, her silhouette was board-stiff.

Tuck sent her a more open glance. "You don't like this, do you?"

Nicole started, as though coming awake. "Pardon?"

"This whole setup. You don't like it."

She looked at the man behind the wheel. "No, I don't like it." She studied Tom for another moment, then returned her eyes to the road. "Have you done this before?"

"Not exactly," he admitted.

"Scott said you have experience in all phases of law enforcement."

"I've gone undercover before, just not to this extent. Doubt if too many people have gone to this extent," he added dryly.

"I keep wondering if it's really necessary," Nicole said with some bitterness. "I'm probably going to lose my job over it."

Tuck sent her another glance. "What do you do?"

"I'm the purchasing agent for the Monte Carlo."

"I'm impressed."

"Well, don't be. I'll probably have to start over as a clerk."

Tuck's lips tightened. He could lay all sorts of lies on her, but the fact was that right now no one could predict the outcome of this case.

"What I don't understand," Nicole said in that same bitter tone, "is why they're sending me so far away. Why not L.A.? Or Phoenix? At least we wouldn't have to drive for days."

"We'll be there before tomorrow night," Tuck answered.

"Meaning you're planning to drive straight through. Great," Nicole said disgustedly. "I can't think of anything I'd rather do for twenty-four hours than ride, ride, ride."

Tuck sent her a cold glance. "You probably have a right to gripe, but I don't want to hear it. Complaining isn't going to do one damn bit of good. And it won't take twenty-four hours. Something under twenty is more like it."

Nicole sat up straighter and gave this unsympathetic, incompassionate jerk a really good look. At the house she'd been so harried and confused she had barely acknowledged their introduction and only vaguely registered his appearance. Staring hard in the faint light from the dash dials, she saw a profile that looked cut from granite, with just about the same amount of warmth.

She'd had her fill of officious, overbearing behavior. From the moment she had made that call to Detective Harper about what she'd seen the night of the Buckley murders, someone had been breathing down her neck, telling her what she could and couldn't do, mercilessly replanning her life—frightening her away from windows, for God's sake—praising her courage one minute and in the next acting as though she hadn't a brain in her head or wouldn't know how to use it if she did.

"If you don't like complaining, you're the wrong man for this job," she said with all of the anger she'd been feeling for days now, anger that she had repressed with great effort. "I will complain about anything and everything that rubs me wrong, Tom King, or whatever your name is, and I don't particularly give a damn how you take it. I'm not here because I want to be and..."

"And you think I am?" Tuck shouted suddenly. "Well, think again!"

They fell silent, each of them startled by how quickly and fiercely their anger had flared. But though Nicole became slightly calmer, defiance was running through her veins, hot and heavy.

"If you didn't want this job, why did you take it?" she questioned acidly. "Or was it forced on you?"

Tuck smirked. "There's all kinds of force, lady. All kinds."

"And I'm sure you know them all," Nicole drawled with exaggerated sarcasm.

"Because I'm a cop?" Tuck laughed humorlessly. "I'm surprised a solid citizen like yourself would make disparaging remarks about cops."

"I was speaking of only one cop, Mr. King. And while we're being so nice and friendly with each other, let's stop one portion of this ridiculous charade. My name is Nicole Currie, and I will not answer to Cheryl."

Tuck muttered a curse. "I've got a damned good notion to turn this car around and drop you off on Joe Crawford's doorstep."

Nicole's chin came up. "Why don't you do that, Officer King? I'm sure Captain Crawford would welcome us both." Her voice became less strident. "Tell me your real name. I can't stand this cloak-and-dagger idiocy. For this thing to work, we're going to have to trust each other. I've trusted you with my real name, and I would appreciate the same courtesy from you."

Tuck drove on, saying nothing for a long time. Nicole finally turned away with a long-suffering sigh. "This is going to be a miserable experience, and I pray to God our association is extremely short-lived," she said wearily.

Several miles went by. "It's Tuck," he said low and tensely. "Tuck Hannigan. In front of anyone else, we're Cheryl and Tom King, understand?"

Nicole's head slowly came around. "Understood, and thank you. Do you know that because of that small piece of information I have more confidence in you?"

He was waiting for his name to sink in. If she'd read the papers or watched the evening news on television six weeks back, she had to have heard it. As for her having more confidence in him, he couldn't care less. The one thing that wasn't going to happen during this job was the two of them getting chummy. He had enough problems of his own to sort through without adding the complication of a personal relationship. He'd just as soon keep this whole thing as *impersonal* as possible.

However, there was one aspect of this fiasco that needed discussion. He spoke tonelessly. "We're going to be posing as Tom and Cheryl King. What we have to decide is how we happen to have the same last name." Nicole turned her head to watch him. "There are several options. I'm sure you can figure out what they are."

Nicole cleared her throat. "Uh, how about brother and sister?"

"That might work. So could pretending to be cousins. But if we're both supposedly single people, we might draw some unwanted attention."

"You mean, like a woman getting interested in you."

"Or a man thinking he'd like to know you better. We're going to avoid people as much as possible, but my professional opinion is that we would be less noticeable as a married couple."

Nicole started chewing on her poor thumbnail again. Posing as this man's wife would entail what? "Um...how far would we have to go to prove our marital status?" she asked uneasily.

He sent her a disgusted look. "We won't be sharing the same bed, if that's what you're thinking, so relax. This is strictly a job to me, strictly business." He drew a breath and retracted some of his anger. "Look, in front of other people we'll have to act as though we know and like each other. That's as far as it'll ever have to go. Understand?"

"Yes," she said quietly, though her nervous system was anything but calm. She leaned her head against the cool window of the door. God, how had she gotten herself into this unholy mess? She had never, ever had anything to do with police officers and the law; there'd never been any reason. She'd never even been to court for a traffic ticket, and now she was going to have to appear as a witness in what would probably be a sensational murder trial. Her own life was in danger, just for being a good citizen.

Tears stung her eyes and nose, and she lifted her head away from the window to go into her purse for some tissues.

Tuck caught on that she was crying and trying to keep it quiet. Keeping his eyes on the road, he pretended not to notice. Still, he felt some sympathy for Nicole Currie. The population seemed to be divided, one portion committing the crimes, the other attempting to lead a good and decent life. When those two segments overlapped in any way, there was always trouble. Nicole hadn't asked for trouble; she had merely stumbled into it. But if the decent side of society never got involved, the crime rate would rise at an even more rapid rate than it was doing in every city and town across the country. The police *needed* people like her, folks who called in to report odd or unusual occurrences. Many a criminal had been brought down because of a simple telephone call from a conscientious citizen.

Of course, few were asked to give up weeks of their life as Nicole was doing. Yeah, he felt sorry for her, but what good would saying so do? She had her self-pity, he had his.

His mouth thinned. Was that what was causing the constant ache in his gut, self-pity? Was self-pity the same as regret? Remorse? And why should he feel any remorse? He had undoubtedly saved the life of that convenience store clerk.

Tense again, he pulled out a cigarette and lit it. Nicole gave him a look. "Must you smoke?"

His answer was to roll down his window about six inches.

She turned her head in disgust. Tuck Hannigan might be a good cop, but he was not a nice guy. Pity his wife or girlfriend, she thought. If he had one.

For some reason his name began tweaking her memory. Tuck Hannigan . . . Tuck Hannigan. She'd heard it before, but how? Where?

And then it came to her. Sergeant Tucker Hannigan had been in the news for killing two men in a convenience store holdup! She sent him a furtive glance, wondering how he felt about that, wondering, too, if he did have a wife and maybe kids. When he wasn't on duty, was he a nicer person? Did he laugh and converse and do ordinary things for fun?

It was hard to imagine him smiling and relaxed. He was the most rigidly controlled person she'd ever met. He'd said this was just another job to him, so how did he view her? Probably as a nuisance, she thought resentfully. Certainly he wasn't treating her as a living, breathing woman with a personality and a brain.

To hell with him. Feeling around for levers down at the right of her seat, she was relieved to find one that released the seat back. It fell back suddenly, causing Tuck's head to jerk around. "What're you doing?"

"Getting comfortable," she retorted, lying back and closing her eyes. She hadn't had a good night's sleep since the onset of this fiasco, and every cell in her body ached with exhaustion. She was asleep in seconds.

Tuck drove through the black night thinking and smoking. Sometimes he only smoked and watched the road. Catching sight of a pair of headlights in the rearview mirror, he slowed down. The vehicle was moving fast, and it soon caught up with him and then passed him doing at least eighty. It was a white sports car and he jotted down the license plate number when it was visible in his own headlights.

The road was monotonous. He passed through the towns of Beatty, Scotty's Junction and Goldfield, and finally approached Tonopah, which was a good two hundred miles out of Vegas. Needing gas, he pulled into a brightly lighted truck stop.

Nicole sat up. "Where are we?"

"Tonopah. I'm getting gas. If you need to use the facilities, do it now."

"What time is it?"

"Around two."

"I'm hungry."

Tuck looked around. There were half a dozen eighteen-wheelers parked with their motors idling, two more at the diesel pumps, and a smattering of cars and pickups parked near the restaurant. No sign of the white sports car.

"Get something to go," he said brusquely. "Do you have money?"

"Yes. Would you like something to eat?"

"Coffee will do. Black, no sugar. Make it a large. And don't waste time."

They got out and went inside, Tuck to the gas attendant to pay in advance for the gas, and Nicole to the ladies' room. She looked at herself in the mirror and felt depressed. Tired, dejected eyes looked back at her.

Dampening a paper towel with cold water, she held it to her eyes for a few minutes. Then, remembering Tuck's domineering "don't waste time," she used the commode, washed her hands and hurried to the restaurant. Sitting at the counter, she put in her order with a weary-looking waitress.

Tuck had the car gassed and the motor idling when she came out with two bags. He drove away the second she was in the car, irritating her, though she said nothing about it and dug into the sacks.

"Here's your coffee." She held out a large foam cup. "I also bought an extra hamburger, in case you might want one."

"Maybe I'll eat it later. Just leave it on the seat."

No "Thanks." No sign of gratitude for her thoughtfulness. Nicole's mouth tightened. "You're welcome, Officer Hannigan," she said with piercing sarcasm.

He shot her a dark look. "I only asked for coffee. But if it's so important to you, thank you very much."

He'd spoken sarcastically, too. Nicole had to forcibly stop herself from continuing the impolite conversation, which could only get worse. They should at least try to get along.

Unwrapping her hamburger, she took a bite and found it to be exceptionally good. So was the coffee.

The sedan sped through the night on the dark and lonely road.

"John Harper said we would be staying in Coeur d'Alene." Nicole said, breaking the silence in the car.

"Not in Coeur d'Alene. *Near* Coeur d'Alene." Tuck took a swallow of his coffee.

"Near? What does that mean?"

"We'll be staying in a cabin on the lake. Coeur d'Alene Lake."

"Oh, there's a lake."

"A very beautiful lake. Northern Idaho has a lot of beautiful lakes. The whole area is beautiful."

"Then you've been there before?"

"Once . . . a few years back."

Nicole finished her hamburger and wadded up the wrapping. "Who owns the cabin?"

"A close friend of a high-ranking police officer. A friend of my captain, as a matter of fact. The guy who talked me into taking this job."

His cynical tone raised Nicole's hackles. "Sorry to be such a burden, but this certainly wasn't my idea," she snapped.

No, it wasn't her idea, and Tuck felt another spurt of sympathy, which he again kept to himself. Nicole Currie might deserve sympathy, but she didn't need to hear it from him. Before this was over she'd either be a lot tougher than she was now, or she would crumble. He hoped it would be the first.

At Tonopah, Tuck had decided to cut east across Nevada and join up with Highway 93, thereby avoiding the traffic around the Reno and Carson City area. He said nothing to Nicole about it, because he could tell that while she stared almost constantly at the road, it wasn't because she was interested in or even aware of her surroundings. Her worried thoughts were directed toward herself, which he probably understood better than most people would have. It was almost as though they had something in common, which wasn't true when their troubling recent experiences were so diverse. But they both had problems to deal with, and that did seem to give them a little common ground.

The term "common ground" gave Tuck pause. He glanced at his passenger. "We should probably get some sort of story put together for our background." Absently then, keeping one eye on the road, he reached for the hamburger on the seat.

Nicole turned slightly to see him. "Such as?"

"Where we're from, where we met, do we have any family, that sort of thing."

"Oh. Do you think people will ask?"

"Not if I can help it, but it wouldn't do for you to answer a question about our common past one way and me answer it another. We really are going to try to avoid people, but we should be prepared, just in case."

"Fine," she said listlessly. "Tell me what to say. Frankly, my own imagination isn't functioning on high at the present."

"Well . . . let's make us both orphans. Parents dead, each of us being an only child. Um, let's say we met back east, got married, lived in Nevada for a while and decided to try Idaho. That would explain the Nevada plates on this car."

"Where back east?"

"Ever been in the east?"

"Only between flights when I vacationed in Europe. But I've been in Texas, the Abilene area."

"That'll work. I've been there, too. Forget the east, and tell people, if they're nosy enough to ask, that we met in Abilene."

After passing through the small town of Warm Springs, there was a long stretch of vacant road through Railroad Valley. Tuck hadn't seen a car in a good half hour when his own began acting up.

Nicole noticed the sputtering of the engine. "What's wrong?"

"Don't know. Maybe the fuel line." Scowling, Tuck pumped on the accelerator and the engine evened out. A breakdown out here wouldn't be funny. The next town of any size was Ely, still more than a hundred miles away. He might come upon a service station before Ely, but on this road in the middle of the night there wasn't much chance of a mechanic hanging around hoping for a customer.

Every few minutes the engine sputtered and coughed again. Nicole had started listening for it and Tuck was getting a little more tense each time it happened.

"What if it stops running out here?" Nicole said worriedly. There wasn't another car in sight, not even a distant light signifying human habitation.

Tuck's jaw was clenched. "Just pray it doesn't," he muttered. He had the feeling the damned engine was going to die any second, and he wished he had stayed on Highway 95, which had more towns and traffic than this road.

Then he squinted at the lights he saw ahead. "There's something coming up," he said. Since there wasn't a town marked on his map, he figured it might be a ranch. To his surprise, it was a gas station and a small motel. The gas station was closed for the night, and he supposed so was the motel. But they each bore lights on tall poles, the name of the motel spelled out in neon.

He pulled the bucking car into the parking area of the buildings. Nicole frowned at the dark and silent service station. "I don't think you're going to get any help at this place."

"Not till morning," Tuck said. "Wait here." Getting out, leaving the engine idling—wheezingly—he stalked to the door of the motel office.

In the car Nicole sighed and laid her head back against the seat. Things just kept getting worse. Not more than a week ago she was a reasonably happy woman with a challenging job, some good friends, and a home she liked and enjoyed. Now here she was in the middle of nowhere, in a pitch-black night, running from killers, with a man she neither knew nor liked, and with a broken-down car in the bargain.

Tuck read the small sign above a button. Ring Buzzer For Late Night Service. He looked around. The motel had about seven units and there were only three cars parked in front of three doors. He pushed on the button.

Almost at once he heard movement from inside. The office lights flashed on, then a sleepy-eyed, middle-aged man in an undershirt and a pair of dark pants with suspenders opened the door.

"I need a room," Tuck said flatly.

"Come in." The man left the door hanging open and walked around a counter. He shoved a card and a pen at Tuck. "Fill it out."

Tuck picked up the pen. "Do you have a room with two beds?"

"The only room I have left has one bed. But it's queen-size."

"Okay." Tuck filled in the blanks and laid down the pen.

The man handed him a key. "Room number six. That'll be forty dollars."

"Forty?" Seemed pretty high for a squalid little motel like this.

"Forty," the man confirmed.

Tuck dug out two twenties and handed them over. "What time does the gas station open in the morning?"

"Around eight."

"Do they have a mechanic?"

"Not regular. But they got a guy on call."

"What about food? Is there a café or something nearby?"

"Just across the road."

Tuck glanced out the door and saw a squat little structure without lights. "Thanks."

Carrying the key, he walked outside. The office lights immediately went off behind him. He headed for the car and got in.

"Got a room for the rest of the night," he said while driving toward room number six.

Nicole gave him a startled look. "*One* room?"

"We're married, remember?" he said dryly.

"I hope it has two beds."

"It doesn't."

She stiffened. "Well, where are *you* going to sleep?"

He shot her a dirty look and pulled the car to a stop. "Bring in only what you have to."

Opening the trunk of the car, he hauled out the smallest of his suitcases. "Which one of yours do you want?"

"I'll get it myself," Nicole answered sullenly.

Tuck shrugged. "Suit yourself."

Together, each with a small suitcase, they walked to the door of room number six. Tuck inserted the key and unlocked the door, then pushed it open and felt around for a light switch.

The room was plain and drab but appeared to be clean. As the man had said, it had a queen-size bed. Tuck set down his suitcase. "In case you're interested, the gas station opens at eight. They have a mechanic on call, so with any luck at all we should be rolling again before noon. In the meantime, get some sleep."

Nicole was staring at the bed. One bed. "I am not sharing a bed with you," she said frostily.

"Then sleep in the damn chair." Tuck yanked off the bedspread, rolled it into a tube and placed it down the center of the bed. "I get the side facing the door. Use the other, if you want. Believe me, lady, your chastity is in no danger from me. Even if I was so inclined, which I'm not, I'm too damn tired to do anything about it." He disappeared into the bathroom, closing the door behind him.

Three

___

Nicole stood there tired and drained. Sharing a motel room with a man she had met no more than five hours ago was affronting, even if he had rather cleverly devised a barrier down the middle of the bed. Setting her suitcase on the floor, she went to a chair and wearily sat down. Tears were very close, burning her eyes and throat and making her head feel tight and achy. The room, though plain and outdated, seemed clean enough, except for the carpet, which was dingy from age and hard usage.

What was she doing here? The question hit her be-numbed brain without mercy. She should be home, in her own bed. She thought of all the postcards and notes she had written to her friends, and her lips clamped together in a thin line. Some of them would accept her brief message without question, but there were a few who might have a *lot* of questions. For one thing, the only close family she had was her mother, who lived in Florida. There were a handful of aunts, uncles and cousins scattered across the country, but Nicole's nearest and dearest friends knew that she didn't stay in touch with her distant relatives. "Family emergency" was a pretty vague message and apt to raise more questions than it answered.

As for her mother, Nicole had ignored John Harper's orders and written Jane Currie a letter. She'd tried to make it one of her normal letters, with only a few lies about a business trip for the Monte Carlo, knowing that a postcard with a ridiculous message would only alarm the older woman. The letter would buy her some time with her mother, Nicole felt, and maybe this mess would come to a head before Jane *did* become alarmed.

The bathroom door swung open and Tuck walked out. Seeing Nicole in a forlorn heap on the chair, he squared his shoulders to forestall another bout of sympathy.

"I'm going outside for a minute."

Her eyes lifted to his and for a moment, the first time really, their gazes connected. A peculiar tingling traveled Nicole's spine, a discomfiting sensation. Turning her head, she nodded. He walked past her and out the door.

Sighing despondently, she got to her feet, picked up her case and went into the bathroom.

Tuck unscrewed the bulb in the light fixture next to the door, then stood in the dark and scanned the area. Everything was silent and he felt none of the wariness he normally did when faced with danger.

Going to the car, he quietly opened the driver's door, got his gun from under the seat, locked the car and returned to tighten the bulb before entering the motel room. There was a dead bolt and a chain on the door, and he used both. Then, placing his holstered gun—and his pack of cigarettes—on the nightstand, he kicked off his boots and stretched out on top of the blanket on his side of the bed. Yawning, he rubbed his eyes. He was tired through and through, and a few hours of sleep seemed like a gift.

Turning on his side, with his back to the tube of bedspread, he shut his eyes.

Nicole opened the bathroom door and turned off the light at the same time. The lights were still on in the bedroom and Officer Hannigan was already in bed. Or rather, he was on the bed, his back to her, fully clothed except for his boots.

Her gaze went from the chair to the vacant side of the bed, back and forth several times. It was no contest, she finally decided. She had to lie down and if Hannigan could sleep in his clothes, she could damn well sleep in hers.

"Turn off the lights."

"Oh! I thought you were sleeping." Nicole went to the light switch by the door and flipped it off. The room was instantly pitch-black, and she had to feel her way to her side of the bed.

But once there and lying down, she heaved a sigh of pleasure. She had worried about falling asleep, but she was dead to the world in three minutes.

Only half-awake, Tuck reached for a cigarette. Then he remembered who was sleeping on the other side of that mound of bedspread and pulled his hand back. Sitting up, he put his feet on the floor and checked his watch: 7:15 a.m. Standing, he headed for the bathroom and a shower.

Nicole began to stir. The shower was running. Suddenly recalling where she was, her eyes jerked opened and she sat up. Hannigan's side of the bed was vacant. Then she spotted the gun on the nightstand. Gnawing at her bottom lip, she stared at the black leather holster and the weapon. She hated guns and was on the political side of much stricter gun control.

But Hannigan was a cop, and cops had to carry weapons.

Tom King... Tuck Hannigan. And she was supposed to be Cheryl King, his wife. God, had ever a more mismatched couple run into each other? He was rude, cold, and had the compassion and sense of humor of a rock. She had never liked people of his ilk, much preferring those who

laughed at silly jokes and themselves. Hannigan was so up-
tight he probably never smiled let alone laughed.

Getting off the bed, Nicole walked over to the window,
opened the short drapes a crack and peered out. The sun was
bright, making the morning air glisten. Across the street was
a wood-sided building with a simple, painted sign: Café. She
smiled. The no-name café was a welcome sight. A cup of
good, hot coffee was exactly what she needed.

Tuck came out of the bathroom. "Get away from the
window."

Nicole whirled around. "I only had the curtains open a
crack." She registered his damp hair, shiny jaw and clean
shirt. It dawned on her then that he was unusually good-
looking. Tall and long-legged, with a lean but muscular
build, and a handsome, brooding face. Her lips pursed because she didn't want to think him good-looking. He wasn't
just a man, he was her protector, and a damned rude one,
to boot.

Tuck set down his suitcase. "I'm going over to that café
and get us some breakfast. What would you like?"

"Why can't I go?"

"Because you can't. What do you want to eat?"

"Must you be so rude?"

"Rude?" He looked away for a moment then returned
harder eyes to her. "This isn't a game, lady, and the sooner
you get that through your head, the better we'll get along."

"We'll get along only if I jump to your commands."

He sized her up with a flinty-eyed stare. "That's about it.
Now, tell me what you want for breakfast."

She wanted to say, "Go to hell!" but she had the feeling
that he'd go across the street, fill his own stomach and to
heck with hers.

"Coffee and . . . toast."

"That's all?"

"Orange juice."

Tuck shrugged. "You got it. Lock the door behind me,
and stay away from the window." Out he went.

Obediently, though angry enough to spit, Nicole threw th dead bolt and hooked the chain. "Jerk," she mumbled taking up her suitcase and heading for the bathroom.

They were on the road again by ten. To Nicole's intens annoyance, Hannigan had made her stay in the motel unit— locked in, and away from the window, of course—while h saw to the car's repair. Fortunately the problem was easy t fix, though to be honest Nicole wasn't interested enough i what it had been to ask. Her mood was growing blacker b the hour, and what really bugged her was that Officer Han nigan didn't even seem to notice. Was she invisible, or what

The miles of central Nevada sped past, miles in whic Tuck said not a word. Finally, Nicole could take no more.

"Are you always this nice?" she asked in an acid tone.

"What?" His eyes left the road to send her a frownin look.

"I said, are you always this nice?"

He looked at the road again. "I'm not here to entertai or amuse you."

She put on a exaggeratedly surprised expression. "N kidding! Boy, you sure could have fooled me."

"What do you want?"

"What do I want? Well, let me see. I want this car goin in the opposite direction. I want to be at my desk instead o heading north. I want..."

"I didn't put you in this situation."

"Neither did I, dammit! Not intentionally," she added so frustrated and furious she marveled that steam wasn' rolling out of her ears. "Why did they pick you for thi job?"

"Meaning, you'd rather have someone else? How do yo know? Maybe I'm the nicest guy on the force."

"Oh, please."

Tuck shook his head, plainly displaying disgust. "I'm no going to argue with you. Save your gripes for someone else."

"If I *ever* see anything else suspicious, rest assured that the police won't hear about it," she said with distinct bitterness.

"Wonderful attitude," Tuck muttered.

"Well, how would you like to be banished from your own home?"

"If it brought down two killers, I'd like it just fine."

She sent him a dirty look. "*You* probably would."

"Look, hasn't it occurred to you that this little trip could be saving your life? Harper probably told you something like that, didn't he?"

"Yes," she said sullenly. Remembering how the dark Lincoln had slowed down as it drove past her car that night, she shivered. The police were right and she was wrong, but why did they have to stick her with a coldhearted, hard-nosed, inconsiderate jerk like Tuck Hannigan?

A side glance caught his granite profile, irritating her all over again. She wanted to ruffle his feathers. Under that inch-thick layer of cop skin had to be a human being.

"Wasn't your name in the papers a while back?" she asked.

Tuck heaved a sigh; she had finally remembered. "Yeah, it was. But I don't want to talk about it, so just drop it."

"You really enjoy giving orders, don't you?" Her mouth twisted. "And I really hate taking them."

"So I've noticed." He sent her a hard look. "But you will take them. When I say move, you move. When I say stop, you stop. And I don't care if there are people around or not. There's a reason behind every order I give you, and I'm not going to waste time explaining every word I say."

"Oh, really? Telling me to drop a subject of conversation is important to this . . . this fiasco?"

"No, but my life isn't open for discussion."

"I suppose mine is, though."

"If it pertains to this job, yes. Otherwise, no."

Nicole folded her arms and stared broodingly out the side window. This was high country, with vast stretches of bar-

ren, sage-covered land. Because there was nothing else to do
Nicole reached for the atlas she'd seen lying on the back
seat, flipped the pages to the one of Nevada and began co
ordinating their location with the map. The mountains she
could see coming up were the White Pine Mountains. Be
hind them were the Monitor Range, the Toquima Range and
the Shoshones. It looked to her like they were only abou
forty miles out of Ely. That was good, because she needed
to find a rest room.

Laying the atlas on the seat between them, she said her
piece. "I need to stop at the first gas station or restaurant we
come to."

He shot her an annoyed look. "Already?"

"Would you like a detailed explanation?" she asked with
saccharine sweetness. "Or may I keep the personal aspects
of my life private?"

"Keep any damned thing you want private. Do you hear
me asking questions about your personal 'aspects'?"

"Well, thank you very much, Mr. Congeniality," she said
with heavy sarcasm.

"You're not the greatest traveling companion, either
lady."

Anger rose in Nicole like steam billowing from a vat of
boiling water. What she wouldn't like to tell this overbear
ing jerk! Clamping her lips shut to stop herself, she turned
her face to the side window.

Tuck's stomach was tight with resentment. Joe had pulled
a fast one on him. *She's a nice woman. You'll like her.* Yeah,
right. If Nicole Currie was nice, he was the tooth fairy. So
far on this trip she'd wallowed in self-pity, bitten his head
off several times, and argued against every one of his in
structions. "Orders," she called them. Why, oh, why, had
he fallen for that "cushy job" line of Crawford's? Right
now he could be peacefully driving along by himself, going
somewhere to be alone and think his own problems through
Instead he had this . . . this emotional female on his hands.

He had put on his dark sunglasses for driving, and out of the corner of his eye he took a look at his passenger. Without that resentful expression on her face she would be prettier than average. He liked her short hairstyle, which was unusual as he normally preferred long hair on women. But the cut fit Nicole's features. Like himself, she had put on a clean top with last night's jeans. Today she was wearing a sleeveless red knit shirt with a V-neck. There was a delicate gold chain around her creamy throat and small gold earrings in her ears. She had put on makeup, too. Not a lot, he would swear, just a little blusher and some lipstick. Also, she must have used a few dabs of that same perfume he'd noticed last night, because the scent was faintly in the air.

His gaze returned to the road and stayed there. She might be pretty and she might smell good, but they were not going to be friends. Acquaintances, eventually, probably, but he wasn't looking for a female friend, particularly in this situation.

"There's a truck stop ahead," Nicole stated.

"I see it."

Tuck studied the traffic around the truck stop and his heart skipped a beat. The white sports car that had passed him last night was at a gas pump. He scanned the area for its driver and decided the person must be inside the building.

Wheeling into the truck stop, he parked next to the restaurant. Leaving the engine idling, he turned in the seat. "I'm going in to check things out. You wait here."

Nicole's eyes widened. "But I need..."

"I said, wait here. If everything's all right, you can go in."

She drew an exasperated breath, which Tuck didn't hear as he was already out of the car and heading for the building.

At the counter there was a line of people—two men and three women—waiting to pay for their purchases. Tuck hung back and looked them over, as one by one they paid for gas or miscellaneous items and walked out.

A long-legged blonde wearing white shorts and a tight yellow T-shirt got into the sports car, gunned the engine and took off.

Tuck went outside and back to his car. "Okay, you can get out now," he said, sliding behind the wheel.

"Thank you very much," Nicole said waspishly, opening her door and hurrying into the building.

Lighting a cigarette, Tuck rolled down his window and thought about that sports car. Its driver being a woman meant nothing. In fact, it would be pretty smart of Lowick to send a woman to tail him and Nicole, but that would mean that Lowicki had somehow learned of the department's plans to protect Nicole outside of Nevada, which only a handful of cops were supposed to know.

Seeing that car twice was probably only coincidence, Tuck thought, though the scowl on his face wouldn't quite go away. Tossing his cigarette out the window, he grabbed the atlas to study the Nevada map. The logical route north from Ely was Highway 93, which was his planned route. But what was best, to take 93 or to cut west on 50 and then take another road north? His scowl deepened. At this rate they'd never get out of Nevada, let alone reach northern Idaho.

Nicole came out and hopped into the car. She had a paper bag with her. Tuck looked at it questioningly.

His expression rubbed her wrong. "It's just some snacks," she said defensively.

"So what did we really stop for?" he asked coldly. "The rest room or snacks?"

"Both," she snapped, although buying some chips and soft drinks hadn't occurred to her until she'd come out of the rest room.

It wasn't until they were several miles out of Ely that she noticed the Highway 50 sign. Frowning, she checked the map and asked, "Why are going west again? Highway 93 goes directly north."

"Just playing it safe," Tuck said.

"Wait a minute. We're zigzagging the state. I thought we'd stay on 95 and you changed directions at Tonopah. Now you're doing it again. Has something happened I'm not aware of to make you waste so much time?"

"In a hurry to get to Idaho?"

"No, I'm not in a hurry," she said sharply. "But I have a right to know what's going on."

Tuck heaved a long-suffering sigh. He didn't want to frighten her, but naturally she'd be curious about his time-consuming route.

"All right, I'll tell you what's going on. I've seen the same car twice, once last night before reaching Tonopah and today it was parked at the truck stop, getting gas."

Nicole gaped at him. "Are you saying that someone is following us?"

"The possibility is extremely remote. I just don't want to take any chances. We're going to cut north on 278."

Nicole looked at the map and located 278. "That road connects with Interstate 80. What are you going to do after that, go east or west?"

"If everything looks okay, I'll probably go east and pick up 225 north at Elko, which will take us through the Duck Valley Indian Reservation into Idaho."

Studying the north-south dimension data on the Nevada and Idaho maps, she sighed. "When we reach the reservation, we'll only be halfway to Coeur d'Alene."

"About that, yes."

"And we still have hundreds of miles to travel in Nevada."

"Yes. But barring further mechanical problems, we'll still reach Coeur d'Alene sometime tonight."

"The *middle* of the night," Nicole said gloomily.

Tuck didn't answer because he was again feeling sympathy for Nicole's plight. There were alternatives to making this long drive, and he should have thought of them when discussing the trip with Captain Crawford. For one thing, they could have chartered a private plane and already be in Coeur d'Alene. Why hadn't Joe thought of that? Why hadn't he?

Then again, Joe Crawford didn't miss much. He probably had considered every possibility and decided driving was their best course. At least Nicole was out of Vegas, which was undoubtedly Joe's primary concern.

Nicole tried to resign herself to the torturous journey. What else could she do, get out and walk? Sighing, she opened the sack and pulled out two cans of soda. "Would you like one?"

Blinking in surprise at her even tone of voice, Tuck nodded. "Yes, thanks."

They stopped for dinner and gas in a little town in Idaho. Tuck was certain now that if the blonde in the white sports car had been tailing them, he had lost her. Unless she knew his destination, that is. There was no way she could have followed his circuitous route without being seen, so if she showed up again, something was damned wrong.

After ordering his meal, Tuck went to the restaurant's pay phone and dialed Captain Crawford's direct line.

"Joe? It's me, Tuck."

"Everything going okay?"

"Our schedule was thrown off by a minor glitch with the car, but we're finally in Idaho. Having dinner in a small town—Riddle. It's about twenty miles across the state line. I'm figuring about eight hours of steady driving to reach Coeur d'Alene. Might be closer to nine with stops."

"That's going to put you in town in the middle of the night."

"My passenger's words exactly," Tuck said dryly.

"How is she holding up?"

"Let's put it this way. You owe me big-time for this 'cushy' job, and I don't plan to let you forget it."

Joe chuckled in his ear. "Aren't you two getting along?"

"You could say that. She's a chronic complainer and doesn't respond kindly to taking orders. Plus, she's not exactly complimentary about police methods."

"You're probably saving her life. Have you said so?"

"In spades. But I guess she's got a right to complain, being uprooted and all. She called it 'banished.' Banished from her home. Anyway, I'm just checking in, as you instructed. One question, Joe. You said this was all pretty hush-hush. Any chance of a leak?"

"Why?"

"I saw the same white sports car twice, on two different highways. It's probably coincidence, but run this license number for me." Tuck recited the plate number.

"Do you want to hold on while I do it?"

"No, my supper's getting cold. Probably wouldn't mean anything to me anyhow. Keep it in mind, though, and let me know if it means anything on my next call."

"Will do, Tuck. Take care."

Once it was dark, Nicole found her head nodding every few minutes. She wanted to stay awake. Hannigan was a good driver, she had decided, but he had to be as tired as she was. Every so often she asked, "Are you getting sleepy?"

His answer was always the same, a flat, rather disgruntled no. Finally he added, gruffly, "Stop worrying. I'm not going to fall asleep and run into something."

There was a lot more to "run into" in Idaho than in Nevada, although there were still long stretches with little population. But without question there were more cars on the road and more towns.

He was paying her no mind whatsoever, Nicole noted irately. Not unless she spoke. When she was silent, Hannigan sat behind that wheel as though he were the only one in the car. Her glance slid his way and her eyes narrowed in circumspection. What was he thinking? What was he like when not on duty? His rugged good looks bothered her, which in turn annoyed her. Thinking him good-looking was irritating when she didn't like him in the least. They had been together for more than twenty-four hours and he hadn't smiled once. Did he think a simple smile would diminish his control over her and the situation?

Sighing heavily, she laid her head back against the seat. They were going to arrive in Coeur d'Alene very late. He must know how to locate the lake cabin, though he hadn't given her the courtesy of explaining exactly where it was.

She couldn't stop herself from expanding that thought. "Have you been to the cabin before?"

"Pardon?"

"The cabin we're going to be staying at. Have you been there before?"

"No."

"But you know where it is."

"I have a map. A drawing."

"Might be hard to find in the dark," Nicole said with some sarcasm.

"I'll find it." He hoped that was true. It had been four, five years since he'd been in the Coeur d'Alene area, and they were coming in from the south, on Highway 95, a road that he couldn't remember being on during his previous visit. Once in the city, he'd have to stop and get his bearings, he realized. Then he'd figure out Joe's hand-drawn map.

It was almost three in the morning when they finally saw the lights of Coeur d'Alene.

"Thank God," Nicole mumbled, her voice thick with exhaustion.

Tuck remained silent, though he felt the same. He kept driving until he reached a well-lighted area, which, he saw, was a large hotel complex. Pulling into the parking lot, he stopped.

"Are we staying here for the rest of the night?" Nicole asked hopefully. It was a beautiful place, and right on the lake. She could almost visualize an elegant room and a comfortable bed.

Tuck was digging into his wallet. "No. I'm checking the map for directions to the cabin." Turning on the overhead light, he studied Joe's drawing.

Nicole yawned. "If I don't get to a bed very soon, I'm going to pass out."

Ignoring her, he kept peering at the drawing until he understood it. Then he got the car moving again.

"We'll be there in about thirty minutes," he said. It was an estimate, a guess. But he knew the way now, and it shouldn't take long.

The lights of the city were soon behind them. They were on a two-lane road that was black as ink. Longingly, Nicole looked back at the city. She would give almost anything she had to stay in town rather than in a cabin that was obviously miles from civilization.

"Damn," she whispered, too tired to even cry.

Four

Tuck was driving slowly, watching intently for the sign designated on Joe's map. The road curved with the terrain, in and out and around, with mountains on one side and the lake on the other. A swath of moonlight seemed to divide the dark water. An occasional dock or buoy light felt like a friend in the black night. A few times in the trees on his right he spotted dim night-lights, belonging, undoubtedly, to a cabin or house. Actually he was surprised that the perimeter of Lake Coeur d'Alene had so much evidence of residency. He'd honestly thought Joe's friend's cabin would be isolated and a good distance from any neighbors. His impression was becoming much different.

Nicole, on the other hand, saw little beyond the heavy forest on their right and the deep, dark water on their left. Bleary-eyed, she noticed only a few of the dock lights.

The road curved away from the lake until Tuck realized there was land between it and the water. "There it is," Tuck muttered under his breath as he spotted a wood sign with

Mathison painted on it. Making the turn onto a dirt driveway, he cautiously wound through the trees. And then he saw it. The cabin. "We're here," he said, breathing a relieved sigh.

The headlights shone on a varnished log structure with a wide front porch. Nicole peered at the building, wondering if she had the strength to make the short trek from car to cabin.

Tuck killed the engine but left the headlights on. "Stay put till I turn on the power. Captain Crawford told me where to find the electricity panel." Carrying a flashlight, he got out and disappeared around the back of the cabin.

Yawning, Nicole laid her head back. If she ever got into a decent bed, she thought, she might sleep for a week.

The next thing she knew Hannigan was shaking her shoulder. "Come on, wake up." Opening her eyes, she saw light beaming from the cabin windows. Numbly she swung her feet around to get out. It was a good thing Tuck was nearby, because her legs gave out and he caught her around the waist and stopped her from sinking to the ground.

"Take it easy," he said. "I'll help you in."

She didn't care that his arm was around her as he guided her to the cabin, up three stairs, across the porch and inside to a chair. He left her there and went back outside. She was sleeping again when he brought in the last of their luggage.

Rubbing his jaw, he stood there and looked at her. Why in hell hadn't she slept during today's long drive? Silly damn female. If he was going to run into something, it could have happened with her watching just as easily as with her sleeping.

Leaving her asleep on the chair, he took a few minutes to explore the cabin. Two bedrooms—each with a connecting bathroom—a large kitchen, a laundry storage room and the main room, where Nicole was parked. He was impressed, as he'd been visualizing a much more rustic place.

Returning to the main room he glanced at Nicole slumped in the chair, then began toting luggage to the bedrooms. Finally it was time to get her out of that chair and into bed.

He touched her shoulder. "Nicole?" She never budged. "Okay," he said grimly. "We'll do it this way." Bending over, he slid his right arm under her legs and his left behind her back. Lifting her from the chair, he started for the bedroom containing her luggage.

She stirred and came partially awake, only to wrap her arms around his neck and lay her head on his shoulder with a soft sigh. Tuck felt a surging in his blood. It was her scent causing it, he told himself; the scent of a woman was usually arousing for a man. Even a tired man.

He laid her on the bed and she instantly curled into a ball. Standing there, he wondered if he should try to awaken her enough to get undressed and under the covers.

Deciding to let her sleep, he found an extra blanket in the closet and spread it over her. Switching off the light, he closed the door, turned off the other lights in the cabin and went to his own bedroom. He placed his gun in the drawer of the nightstand. It took him about two minutes to shed his clothes and crawl into bed.

He was asleep almost before his head hit the pillow.

Tuck awoke to bright sunlight streaming through the bedroom window. He checked his watch: 9:15 a.m. Stretching, he yawned and got out of bed. He wasn't completely rested, but he had to look over the area and couldn't lie in bed all day.

A shower and shave shook the cobwebs from his brain and he dug into a suitcase for clean clothes. In the kitchen he found the coffeemaker and a can of coffee. Putting on a pot to brew, he went outside through the kitchen door, then stopped to admire the tall pines surrounding the cabin. He took a hike around the building, spotted several other cabins in the trees, took note of a small shedlike building all but hidden in a copse of trees and brush behind the Mathison cabin, discovered that the property made a gradual descent to the shore of the lake, then went back inside for that coffee.

Sitting at the table with a cup, he used the wall phone to dial Captain Crawford's private number.

"Joe? We're here."

"Good. Did you see any more of that sports car?"

"No."

"I ran the plate and it's registered to a Jillian Marsden." He spelled out the last name. "Las Vegas address. No record, other than a speeding ticket about six months ago. She appears to be clean, but I've got a man checking her out."

"Thanks."

"How is our friend this morning?"

"Still sleeping."

"How do you like the cabin?"

"It's a nice place. I didn't expect neighbors, though."

"There are cabins and homes all around the lake, Tuck. I wouldn't worry too much about the neighbors. A lot of those places are only used on weekends and such, most of them owned by locals. Now that I know you're there and all right, don't call again unless it's necessary. I'll call you if there's anything going on here you should know."

"Got it." Tuck hung up and sat there sipping his coffee. There were sounds piercing the quiet—motorboats on the lake, he realized. But, damn, it was peaceful here, and it smelled good. The piney odor of the trees was even inside the cabin. A small smile played with his lips. Maybe this *was* a cushy job. For certain Joe couldn't have picked a prettier spot to secrete his witness.

Nicole opened her eyes, looked at her watch and gasped. She had never slept until 1:00 p.m. in her life...and in her clothes, to boot. The room felt hot and she felt sweaty and choked by her clothing. Sliding off the bed, she looked around the room, wondering where its three doors led.

Before trying any of them, however, she needed some fresh air. Opening the window, she took a deep breath and smelled the tang of pine. Then she noticed the trees and the sunshine. "What a gorgeous day," she said softly, suddenly anxious to be outdoors.

But first things first. One door opened onto a closet, one onto a hall, and the third, hallelujah, opened onto a very nice bathroom.

Tearing off her clothes, she turned on the shower.

Tuck was hungry enough to start gnawing bark by the time Nicole made an appearance. His gaze slid over her. She was wearing knee-length blue shorts, a white T-shirt and sandals. Her pretty face touched something within him, ringing a warning bell. They were going to be spending a lot of time together, and admiring her good looks wasn't the smartest way to maintain their unusual relationship.

"There's no food. We've got to drive back to the city and do some shopping," he said brusquely.

She had been all set to say something cheery, but Hannigan's gruff and unfriendly attitude dispelled the impulse.

"Why didn't you just go without me?" Her voice was cool and disdainful.

"I think you know the answer to that question as well as I do. Come on, let's go."

Nicole followed him out the front door, which he locked behind them. "Are you telling me that you are never going to let me out of your sight?" Her gaze swept the area and she stopped in her tracks. "Oh, it's beautiful out here. Look, the lake is right there. And the trees, so many trees."

Her enthusiasm for the beauty of the area matched Tuck's, but he wasn't going to gush with her over anything. Distanced behavior was their best course, and he was determined to maintain it.

"Let's get going," he said gruffly.

Shooting him an irritated look, she trailed him to the car and got in. "Why didn't you wake me? It's ridiculous that you've been hungry for hours while I slept."

Tuck started the engine. "You were exhausted. Don't worry about it, okay? We'll load up on groceries and you can sleep in every morning, if that's what you want."

"I *never* sleep in," she said frostily. "Or I never did before today." Hannigan obviously didn't like her, but there was little sense to them constantly snapping at each other. Lord only knew how long they would be sharing that cabin. She figured they might as well make the best of the situation.

Nicole's tone became less chilly. "I really haven't slept a night through sense I phoned Detective Harper," she said. "Add that to the long trip, and I'm sure that's the reason I was so worn out last night."

They were on the winding road to town and Tuck's mind was mostly on driving. But her reference to phoning Harper raised a few questions. "Captain Crawford never did explain what you saw. He only told me that he had a witness that could place Lowicki and a guy he thinks was Gil Spencer at the scene of the murders."

Nicole was entranced with the scenery. The lake was sparkling in the sunshine, and there were boats and water skiers dotting the large body of water.

"All I saw was two men leaving a building at one in the morning," she said rather absently. "When I read about the double murders at that building in the paper the next morning, I thought I should call Detective Harper. Frankly, it never occurred to me that my information was of any real importance."

"You must have identified Lowicki," Tuck said.

"Well, he has an unusual scar. . . ."

"On his left cheek. What about the other guy?"

Nicole hesitated. "Rather nondescript. Average height, a little overweight, dark hair. I couldn't pick him out in the hundreds of photos John Harper had me look through." Thoughtfully she added, "But the man with the scar was so. . . well, frightening, that I really didn't pay a lot of attention to the other man."

"They didn't see you?"

"I'm positive they didn't." Nicole bit down on her lip for a moment, her brow furrowed. "What they did see was my car. They were driving a dark blue or black Lincoln, and it slowed down as it passed my car, as if they were giving it a thorough once-over."

"They probably were. Probably got the license number, just to play it safe."

"But the Department of Motor Vehicles doesn't give out names and address to just anybody, does it?"

"No, but there are ways," Tuck muttered. Realizing then that he was scaring Nicole, he said no more.

Frowning intently, Nicole stared out the side window at the beautiful, sparkling lake. Even if Lowicki and his companion unearthed her name and address from her license plate, they would never find her here. And if by some slim chance they did figure out where she was, Hannigan would protect her.

Her heart started pounding like a wild thing. How capable *was* Sergeant Hannigan? Did a brooding, sullen attitude indicate anything beyond a cold, unfriendly personality? He had killed two men, she reminded herself, so he wouldn't hesitate to use his gun if necessary. And certainly he was cautious. God, his caution had driven her to the brink several times during their drive north.

She flicked his rock-hard profile a harried glance. Whatever he was, however capable or inept he was, she *had* to put her trust in him. Hannigan was all she had, the only barrier between her and two killers.

Shuddering, she faced front and told herself to stop thinking about it. Not only did she have to trust Hannigan, she had to have faith that Captain Crawford had chosen the right man for the job. Without faith, she could drive herself crazy with worry.

It amazed Nicole that Hannigan could shop with her, decide on the quality and quantity of various food supplies, and still remain so aloof. Ice man, she thought. He was a man without a dram of warmth for the human race or much of anything else, either.

She noticed, though, that he saw everything, although his eyes never seemed to dart nor did he appear to be ostensibly alert. He was wearing khaki slacks and a short-sleeved tan shirt. They looked like any ordinary couple filling their weekly grocery list.

But Hannigan wasn't at all ordinary, she realized. She was becoming somewhat attuned to his behavior, his stern expressions and terse comments. Easily he was the handsomest man in the supermarket they'd chosen, though she was positive he couldn't care less about his looks.

The one thing he couldn't camouflage with common clothing, she decided while they were transferring sacks of food from the cart to the car, was his eyes. Another cop would recognize him as a fellow officer, she would bet. Flinty eyes. Cop's eyes. See-all eyes.

She sighed at the inanity of her thoughts. Hannigan was different than anyone she'd ever met, and that was the long and the short of it. Cop's eyes, indeed. Her imagination was running wild.

"Do you want to cook or should I?" Tuck asked while wolfing down a banana. The food was put away, except for the ground beef and salad greens slated for their dinner.

"Makes no difference to me," Nicole replied evenly. It didn't surprise her that he could cook, though it did birth an interesting question. "Do you do the cooking at home?"

"Since I live alone, yes."

"Oh, you're not married."

He didn't bother to comment on that remark. "I'll cook and you clean up."

Nicole's left eyebrow shot up. Was she the maid here, or what? "*I'll* cook and *you* clean up."

He tossed the banana peel into the trash can under the sink, then leaned his hips against the counter and folded his arms. "I've got a better idea. You cook *and* clean up. I'll do the other chores, like bringing in wood for the fireplace."

"I hardly think we need a fire in this weather." What a con artist!

"Yeah, but I like wood fires, and it cools down at night. It was plenty cool last night when we got here, only you were too out of it to notice."

She waved her hand in disgust. "Do what you want. I suspect you usually do. I'll make dinner and I'll do the dishes, too. Just don't stand there and watch me."

"'Watching you' is what I'm being paid to do." It was also a pleasure, he was beginning to realize uneasily. She moved like a woman, which was a ludicrous observation since she *was* a woman. But there was something special about the grace of her movements. Very feminine and very sexy. He shouldn't be noticing.

She turned with snapping eyes. "Get the hell out of the kitchen, Hannigan, or you can do *all* the cooking and *all* of the cleaning up."

He grinned, shocking Nicole to speechlessness. He *could* smile, and what a smile it was. Gorgeous white teeth flashed at her, and the most disarming crinkles appeared at the corners of his eyes.

But the grin disappeared almost immediately. "Guess *you're* giving the orders today, huh?" With that reminder of her resentful remarks against giving and taking orders yesterday, he walked out.

Nicole stood there recalling his grin. There was a peculiar sensation in the pit of her stomach, one that definitely shouldn't be there. Trying to ignore it, she got busy with dinner. But her brain wasn't very cooperative and she couldn't stop herself from thinking about her rather pitiful love life.

She was thirty-two years old and there had been several men in the past who had been important for a while. But it had been almost two years since her last sexual relationship, even though there had been plenty of opportunities for

casual, overnight sex. Most of the men she'd been dating—
fewer and fewer over the years—thought that an evening
together—dinner, dancing, a movie or what have you—
should end up in his place or hers. She didn't agree, which
usually forestalled a second date. The men who were ego-
tistical enough to think a second date would bring her
around were sadly disappointed, which abruptly ended the
relationship.

In a few cases Nicole was disappointed herself. She would
have liked the opportunity to know the man better. There
was one, in particular, Chuck Harding, who also worked at
the Monte Carlo, that she would have liked to date again.
He was fun to be with and good-looking, as well. But after
her second refusal to go to bed with him, Chuck had written her off.

She had tried to explain her point of view, but he really
hadn't given a damn about her feelings. She knew he
thought of her as a prude, and short of throwing herself at
him there was no way of getting his attention again. All he
wanted was sex from any woman he dated, an attitude she
simply couldn't accept.

Now, here she was, trapped in a cabin with a man who
had made her feel like a woman with one smile. Dangerous
business, she cautioned herself. *Very* dangerous. While
Hannigan was "watching" her, she had better watch her
step around him. Anything else would be foolhardy and
definitely out of character for her.

Nicole minced onions to mix with the ground beef, which
she shaped into patties and oven-broiled, prepared the green
salad, popped potatoes into the microwave to bake and
boiled two large ears of corn.

Aware that Hannigan was outside wandering around and
seemingly deep in thought, she called out the back door,
"Dinner's ready."

He came in at once. The table was set nicely and the plat-
ters and bowls of food made his mouth water. "Looks

great." After he'd filled his plate and taken a few bites, he realized it *was* great. "You're a good cook."

"It's simple fare, but thanks." A feeling of discomfort invaded Nicole's system. Sitting down to eat with Hannigan felt like intimacy, and there were countless meals ahead of them. An unknown number of days and nights to get through, and he had already let her know that he wasn't going to let her out of his sight. Which meant that he wasn't going to permit her to take the car, for example, and go off by herself, no matter how smothered she might get to feeling by his constant vigilance.

Sighing, she buttered an ear of corn.

"Something bothering you?" he asked.

"Need you ask?"

"You don't like it here."

"This place is beautiful. I like it very much." Her eyes rose to meet his. "But it's really just a prison, isn't it?"

"And I suppose I'm the warden?"

"Aren't you?"

He shook his head. "You have an odd way of looking at things."

"Well, how would you describe the situation?"

They were eating while talking, enjoying the good meal despite the disruptive topic of their conversation.

"You're not in prison," Tuck said gruffly. "There's only one restriction on your activities, and it's that you can't go wandering off by yourself."

"No, you have to go with me." Nicole laid down her fork. "Now, really, do you actually believe anyone in Vegas knows where I am? How could they? I think you're being much too cautious."

Tuck leaned forward. "You really haven't grasped the kind of men we're dealing with, have you? They will go to any extreme to eliminate anyone who can place them at the scene of their crime. They may be the worst kind of criminals there are, but they're not stupid. By now I'd be willing to bet anything that they know everything there is to know about you, including your name, your address and where you work. Don't underestimate them, Nicole.''

A chill went up her spine. ''Okay,'' she said weakly. ''I'll concede to your experience and professional knowledge. But how would they know you brought me to Idaho? Why not Montana, or Florida? Do you see my point? I could be in any one of a million places.''

Tuck thought of that white sports car, which could mean nothing or everything. He'd kept a sharp eye out for it today in town and hadn't seen it. But he had an uneasy feeling about it all the same. For one thing, if Jillian Marsden had any connection to Nick Lowicki and had left Las Vegas at Lowicki's bidding the same night he and Nicole had, then there was a leak in the department, someone who'd caught wind of Crawford's plan to protect his witness and passed it on to Lowicki. If that was the case, Nicole was in grave danger.

On the other hand, that car traveling north on their schedule could be mere coincidence. What it boiled down to was that he wasn't willing to take that chance. Until he knew otherwise, Jillian Marsden's trip north was highly suspect.

Not that he was going to inform Nicole of his suspicions. Obviously she felt relatively safe here, which was good. At least she wouldn't be walking around jumping at every sound and seeing a killer behind every tree. But she was going to have to put up with his cautionary measures, like them or not.

''We're going to play it safe,'' he told her, speaking forcefully enough that Nicole's lips thinned with resentment. ''Sorry if you find that offensive, but that's the way it is.''

They finished the meal in silence. Nicole got up to clear the table and Tuck went outside to smoke. ''Overbearing jerk,'' she resentfully mumbled, watching him through the window above the sink. The kitchen was well-equipped, containing even a dishwasher. Nicole loaded it quickly, wiped down the stove, table and counters, rinsed and dried her hands and then went to her bedroom for some hand lotion.

The sight of her suitcases pained her, but her clothes should be hung in the closet rather than getting more wrinkled by the day. She set to work, but even this chore irritated her. Everything going on irritated her. She should be in her own home, living her normal life, not confined to a cabin in northern Idaho. Confined was the right word, all right. As pleasant as this cabin was and regardless of Hannigan's supposedly expert opinion, it *was* a prison.

Five

Dusk was settling in. Nicole walked through the cabin, looked out the kitchen window and saw nothing of Hannigan. Going to a front window, she spotted him down by the lake. She glared at the lone figure. *He* could take walks by himself, but she couldn't.

Angrily she left the cabin and marched down the hill to where Hannigan was standing. "In case you didn't notice, you left me alone in the cabin. Isn't that exactly what you said would never happen?"

He turned with a cool expression. "Are you mad at something again?"

"Oh, go to hell," she muttered, and took off walking along the shore. Coeur d'Alene Lake was the most beautiful body of water she had ever seen. Heavily forested mountains made a scenic backdrop for the water, which was sparkling silver and gold from the setting sun.

"That's far enough," Tuck said brusquely.

She was about fifty feet away from him, and she turned

with a well-defined scowl. "What do you think is going to happen out here in the open? For crying out loud, you can practically reach out and touch me."

"Come here."

"What for?"

Tuck heaved an impatient sigh. "There's something you need to hear."

Sullenly, Nicole walked back to him. "What is it?"

"It occurred to me that someone could easily reach this place with a boat." As before, he didn't want to frighten her, but she was much too defiant and maybe needed a little scare.

Nicole's eyes darted to the lake. She had thought only of its beauty, certainly not that it provided easy accessibility to the cabin.

"Oh," she said, swallowing the sudden lump of fear in her throat, her gaze returning to Tuck. The twilight made his skin, hair and eyes appear darker than they really were. He looked hard as nails, tough as shoe leather, and unutterably handsome.

Tuck was thinking similar thoughts about his charge. Nicole Currie wasn't just pretty this evening, she was beautiful. Maybe he'd just now noticed how really striking she was, he thought uneasily. But noticing her looks wasn't the only thing on his mind. The fear in her eyes made him want to take her in his arms and tell her to forget what he'd just said, tell her that nothing or no one would ever harm her as long as he drew breath.

He shoved his hands into his pants' pockets to keep from doing something foolish. "Let's go back to the cabin."

Nicole nodded and they started trudging up the hill. She glanced back at the lake with a furrow of concern between her eyes.

"I didn't tell you that to scare you," Tuck said quietly, though it was a most definite lie about something he now regretted. "I just want you to be careful. And watchful."

The evening air was cooling down considerably, but Nicole's shiver wasn't from feeling chilly. It was beginning to sink in, deep and sure, that the danger wasn't all in Hannigan's mind.

"I will be," she said meekly.

Her tone surprised Tuck and he sent her a glance. Wanting to rid her mind of the fear, he said, "This would be a great place for a vacation, don't you think?"

"You mean, if one didn't have to constantly watch for people trying to eliminate you?"

"Uh, yeah. Nicole, try not to think about it."

"Be watchful and careful but don't think about it. That's a tall order, Hannigan."

A speedboat racing along close to the shore drew their attention. They stopped and turned to watch it rushing past, going so fast its bottom barely touching the surface of the water.

"Lots of boats on this lake," Tuck commented casually.

"Yes, lots," Nicole murmured, squinting at the vanishing craft. He wasn't fooling her one bit with his nonchalant remarks. The lake presented accessibility, thus danger. It wasn't something she would have thought of on her own, and now, she could tell, he wished he hadn't mentioned it to her.

They started up the hill again. Nicole's distraught thoughts weren't on the ground, however, and she caught the toe of her sandal on a tree root and found herself falling forward.

A pair of strong arms caught her before she hit the ground. "Take it easy," Tuck said, bringing her upright and on her feet again. But he didn't let go of her. "Are you all right?" His eyes searched hers.

She gulped. Her heart was beating fast—from the near fall, she supposed—and her breathing was a little off kilter. "I—I think so." Why didn't he let go of her? Was he going to kiss her? Her tongue flicked to moisten her lips.

Why Tuck kissed her, he would never know, other than that she was beautiful and sexy and they were alone in the trees. His first kiss was a simple brushing of his lips against hers, but when she didn't object or pull away, he placed his mouth firmly on hers. He was instantly aroused, but what really shook him was the way Nicole was kissing him back. Her arms locked around his waist and her breasts pushed into his chest. Her mouth opened and he felt her tongue. Her response and his own was startling; it was too much, too fast, and he was a damn fool.

He lifted his head, pulled her arms away from his waist and stepped back. "Sorry," he said harshly. "I shouldn't have done that." His brain was heaping curses on his own head. What in hell had gotten into him?

She blinked at him. "I—I knew you were going to kiss me, but I didn't know I was going to kiss you back."

"Neither did I. Come on." The anger he was feeling was for himself, but Nicole couldn't tell the difference. He sounded as though he was blaming her for that kiss.

"It wasn't my doing," she said defensively, trudging beside him. She could still feel the imprint of his mouth on hers, the firm but yielding sensation of his lips and the configuration of his lean, hard body against hers. It was unnerving to realize that she would like to sample another of Sergeant Tuck Hannigan's kisses.

"Who said it was?" Tuck said darkly. "Don't worry. It won't happen again."

Hurt at his hostile attitude, she took off jogging toward the cabin. In retaliation, she hurled back at him, "You're sure right about that!"

Conversely, Tuck slowed his steps. That had been the most stupid thing he'd ever done on a job. They had spent only a few days together and he was already making passes? Had he lost his mind somewhere between Nevada and Idaho?

He sat on the porch steps, staring broodingly at the view of trees and water. He never should have taken this "cushy" job. He could be somewhere by himself right now, not worrying about protecting anyone, and certainly not making a horse's rear end out of himself by kissing a woman whom he shouldn't even *notice* was a woman.

Even though it was early, Nicole went to her bedroom, slipped into a nightgown and crawled into bed. She didn't want to see Tuck Hannigan again tonight. Damn him. He'd kissed her and then acted as though *she* had made the pass.

There was only one gratifying aspect to the bizarre episode: Tuck Hannigan was human after all.

Though Tuck was tired and also went to bed early, he found himself lying there unable to relax. He had already dismissed that kiss; it had been an unexpected mistake and wasn't going to be repeated.

But unnerving questions about himself kept him awake. *Was* he being overly cautious with Nicole's safety? Were his instincts working with the same fine precision that they used to? Was he spooked unnecessarily over that white sports car?

He had changed since those convenience-store killings; was he even a good cop now? But if he wasn't a cop, what was he?

Restless, he got up and wandered through the dark cabin to peer out each of its windows—except for the one in Nicole's room. He had left two lights burning, the one next to the back door and the one that illuminated the front porch. He was positive that Joe Crawford believed he had sent his witness to a place of safety, but it would be a simple matter for someone to approach the cabin via the lake. Joe probably hadn't considered that possibility because he was so certain of the secrecy of his plan.

Tuck wasn't that certain, but he didn't trust his imagination not to play tricks on him. He smirked. What he used to call instinct now felt like imagination. Great, just great.

His eyes narrowed in speculation. Maybe he should take Nicole and get the hell out of here, go somewhere where no one, not even Crawford, would know where they were.

But wouldn't that be overkill? Was he afraid he couldn't handle a couple of thugs if they should suddenly appear? Maybe that was it. Maybe he was afraid now.

His lips tightened into a thin, grim line. He had to prove himself *to* himself. If he ran now, he may as well keep on running, because his career in law enforcement would be over.

He went back to bed, determined to see this through and to protect Nicole at any cost to himself. He *was* still a cop, dammit, and this job was going to prove it.

Nicole awoke in the morning to the sound of rain. It was a lulling, soothing, almost musical sound, and she snuggled deeper into her blankets. Her home in Las Vegas had a tile roof and a two-foot crawl space filled with insulation against the grueling heat of Vegas summers. When it rained in southern Nevada—very seldom—she couldn't hear it in the house. This was lovely, lying cozily in bed with the pattering of raindrops on the roof.

Without cause or reason, her thoughts jumped from rain to that kiss Hannigan had taken last evening. Taken or given. It was difficult to decide whether he'd taken or given when she had kissed him back with such fervor. *Why* had she kissed him back? Certainly she wasn't accustomed to kissing men she didn't like. This whole awful episode was turning her into someone else, a woman she neither knew nor understood.

Reality gradually destroyed her good mood and she threw back the blankets and got up with a disgusted grimace. No more kissing, she vowed, which she would be more than happy to tell Mr. Stiff-Necked Hannigan should he try something again.

After showering and dressing, she made her bed and left her room. The cabin was silent, feeling eerily vacant. She took a breath, ridiculing the sudden fear she felt. Hannigan wouldn't leave without telling her where he was going and when he'd be back. He was probably outside somewhere, dutifully standing guard or performing some other cop activity. She wasn't denigrating his devotion to duty, she merely didn't understand the man who'd taken the job of protecting her.

Sighing, she peered into the kitchen and spotted the pot of coffee on the counter. Pouring herself a cup, she wandered into the main room and then stopped dead in her tracks. Tuck was standing to the side of the window, furtively looking through a pair of binoculars toward the lake.

"Now what?" she asked with rising panic in her voice. "Is someone out there?"

Tuck lowered the binoculars and turned to see her. She looked as fresh as the morning dew, striking in white slacks and a navy top, with her short hair still damp from the shower, and makeup on her pretty face.

He'd been watching a fisherman who had anchored his small boat about a hundred feet from shore. He'd seen the man—he thought it was a man, though with all the rain gear covering his body and head, he couldn't be positive—prepare his fishing line and drop it into the water. It all looked as innocent as a newborn babe, and yet Tuck had to question why the person had chosen that particular spot to do his fishing.

"Just a fisherman," he said evenly.

"He's fishing in the rain?" Nicole started for the window to see the scene for herself.

"Stay back," Tuck said gruffly. "If we can see him, he can see us."

"Is he using binoculars, too?" Nicole asked, her voice underlaid with sarcasm. Even accepting Hannigan's role here, it was irritating to be constantly harangued about one thing or another. *He'd* been looking out the window. Why couldn't she?

"I haven't seen any," Tuck admitted brusquely. "But he's been out there since dawn." What bothered him most was that he couldn't tell if he'd been watching a slightly built man or a woman. "Come around that chair and take a look."

Detouring around the chair would keep her out of sight should anyone be watching the window, Nicole had to acknowledge, albeit resentfully. Since she didn't really resent Hannigan as a cop, she must resent him as a man, she thought while setting her coffee on a table and following his instructions to reach his side. He handed her the binoculars and stepped back.

"Stand exactly where I was," he told her. "You'll be able to see him without him seeing you."

Frowning, Nicole brought the binoculars to her eyes and adjusted the focus. "I see him."

"Is it a man or a woman in that boat?"

Her frown deepened. "He's so covered up with that rain coat and hat, I can't really tell." Lowering the binoculars, she looked at Tuck. "Why do you think it's a woman?"

"Women fish, don't they?"

"I suppose they do, but it's raining."

"What's that got to do with it?"

"Well, I might fish, but I certainly wouldn't do it in the rain."

"Nicole," Tuck said impatiently, "there are people who believe fish take the hook better when it's raining."

"Oh. Well, how would I know that?" She handed him the binoculars. "I think you're making a mountain out of a mole hill. So there's a person out there fishing? So what?"

"Why is he—or she—anchored right in front of this place?" Tuck muttered, taking another look through the binoculars. Not once since he'd first noticed the boat had the person in it turned enough for him to see his or her face. That in itself seemed suspicious.

"Why don't you just close the darn drapes and forget it?" Nicole said. "I'm hungry. Have you eaten?"

"No."

"I'm going to make breakfast." Darting around the chair to keep Hannigan happy, she picked up her cup of coffee and left the room shaking her head. Protectiveness was one thing, obsession was something else. The poor guy—or gal—out there in that boat had no idea a steely-eyed, overly suspicious cop was watching his every move. What on earth could be more innocent than fishing? So what if the person had anchored his boat in front of the Mathison cabin? Maybe that was a good fishing spot. Maybe he or she had caught lots of fish in that spot on rainy days.

What really irked her was that last night Hannigan had gone down to the lake and she had located him by looking through the very window he'd chased her back from this morning. Obviously he was getting even more picky and demanding than he'd been, which seemed almost impossible considering his bossy attitude during that miserably long and exhausting drive to get here.

Well, at least she could look out the kitchen window, she thought while rinsing her cup at the sink to use again with breakfast. Glancing out just to prove she could, her heart nearly stopped. Walking up to the back door was a man.

She ran from the kitchen and stood just inside the main room with her back to the wall next to the doorway. "Tuck," she whispered. "Hannigan," she said louder when it became obvious that he hadn't heard her.

He lowered the binoculars and turned with a scowl. "What?"

"There's a man—" The sudden rapping at the back door eliminated further need for explanation.

Tuck came around the chair with an expression so cold and forbidding, Nicole shivered. "Stay in here," he ordered, and all but ran to his bedroom for his gun, which he shoved into his jeans at the back of his waist. The man had knocked a second time before Tuck finally opened the door.

The man, wearing a bright red rain jacket and hat, had a grin a yard wide. "I'm your neighbor, Jim Tripp. Live right over there." He pointed to the log house Tuck could see in the trees.

"Uh...Tom King." Tuck offered his hand, which Mr. Tripp, an elderly man, heartily shook.

"You and the missus here on vacation?"

Tuck nodded. "A long vacation, we hope."

"Glad to hear it. Pete Mathison hardly uses the place. Be good to have some neighbors for the summer."

Tuck could tell that Mr. Tripp was just itching for an invitation to come inside, meet the "missus," and probably sit around and chat all morning. Under ordinary circumstances, Tuck would have welcomed the chance to make friends with this congenial older man.

But circumstances weren't at all ordinary. "Jim, I'd ask you in but my wife isn't feeling well."

Mr. Tripp's face took on a somber cast. "That's too bad, Tom. Tell her I'm real sorry I missed meeting her this morning. Another time, all right?"

"Yes," Tuck agreed. "Thanks for coming by." As Jim Tripp walked away, Tuck called, "Is there a Mrs. Tripp?"

Jim stopped to smile. "Sure is. Let's all get together for dinner some evening. After this rain lets up we'll have a little barbecue at my place. How does that sound?"

"Sounds fine, Jim, but with Cheryl not feeling well, I can't make any definite plans."

Mr. Tripp's expression again sobered. "Hope it's nothing serious, Tom."

Inspiration hit Tuck. What better excuse could he find to avoid friendly people than his "wife" being laid up for an indefinite period? He spoke solemnly. "She had an operation about a month ago, Jim, and recuperation is going to take time. The doctor said quite a lot of time, to be honest."

"I understand, young man. Well, take good care of her. Let us know if you need anything. We're almost always at home."

"Thanks, Jim. I appreciate it."

Tuck closed the door, then watched at the window until Mr. Tripp had gained the trees separating the two cabins. Nicole came around the door. "An operation?" she drawled with heavy sarcasm.

"It's a good idea, so don't knock it. I don't want us eating barbecue with the neighbors and one of us saying something to ruin our cover."

"You're talking about me. Certainly *you* would never forget yourself and do something so unforgivable."

"I'm talking about both of us."

"Yeah, right," Nicole drawled.

Obviously Hannigan was going to be her only companion during this godawful fiasco. That man, Mr. Tripp, had sounded pleasant and sincere. He wasn't a spy for Lowicki or a hit man sent from Las Vegas to shut her mouth for good. Hannigan was overdoing the protection bit, and she was no more than a prisoner. *His* prisoner.

Angry and resentful, she began opening and then slamming cupboard doors shut after pulling out items for their breakfast. It was then that she noticed the gun stuck in Hannigan's jeans.

"What were you planning to do, shoot the man for being neighborly?" she asked in a voice dripping icicles.

Sending her a look of utter disgust, Tuck walked out of the room, leaving Nicole to simmer and stew by herself.

"Damned woman," he muttered while returning the gun to the drawer of his nightstand. Remembering the fisherman, he bolted to the living room and his former position next to the window.

The boat was gone. Tuck cursed under his breath. He had wanted to see in which direction that fisherman went when he got tired of sitting out there in the drizzle. Giving the drapery pull a yank to cover the window, Tuck thought resentfully that now Miss Smartass Currie could wander the room at will.

She was a real pain in the . . . neck.

* * *

To be factual, Nicole had never before been alone in a house with a man she didn't like and enjoy being with. As the day dragged and the rain didn't stop—she couldn't leave even if it had because of Hannigan's watchful eye—and they barely spoke to each other, she had nothing to do except wander from room to room and wish she were anywhere but here, locked in with a fanatic cop who thought that even friendship with a nice old guy like Jim Tripp was a cardinal sin. Her patience kept getting thinner and thinner until she felt ready to explode.

"Can't you light somewhere?" Tuck grumbled when she'd passed his chair for about the twentieth time.

She stopped pacing to glare at him. "I'm doing nothing that should bother you, so don't bother me, okay?"

Tuck heaved a long-suffering sigh. "Look, this thing has just begun. We're going to be here for God knows how long. Didn't you bring along anything to read? Or why don't you turn on the TV set and watch something? Just stop that infernal pacing."

"How nice for you that you can plop into a chair and do nothing for hours on end. I'm not made that way, Hannigan. I'm accustomed to activity, to responsibility, to conversation. Normal conversation, I might add. You know what that is, don't you? When two people talk? When one introduces a topic and the other responds? It's probably happened once or twice in your life, painful as it undoubtedly was for you."

"You don't want to talk, you want to fight."

She rolled her eyes. "That's precisely the sort of answer I expected to hear from you. Hannigan, is it the job, me, or women in general you dislike so much?"

He got to his feet. "To tell you the truth, lady, I'm not overly fond of any of your choices."

For some reason she felt hurt. "Well, that goes double for me about you!" Whirling, she went to her bedroom and slammed the door behind her.

It was Tuck's turn to pace. Weeks of this would have them both climbing the walls. Why had Joe described this job as "cushy"? Had he figured Idaho would be so safe they could take advantage of the recreation in and around Coeur d'Alene? Actually enjoy the area and all it had to offer? If this was an ordinary situation and they were an ordinary couple on vacation, they could play golf, take their pick of the city's numerous restaurants, rent a boat and explore the lake, even take in some of the nightlife.

Tuck rubbed his jaw thoughtfully. He'd bet anything that was what had been in Joe's mind. Though Joe had said the job would consist only of keeping the witness company, there was a whole lot more to it. From the very start Nicole had been resistant and resentful; keeping her cooped up as he had today was making her even more resentful.

After a few more minutes of thinking it over, Tuck went down the hall and knocked at her door. "Come on out. We're going for a drive."

Her door opened. "A drive where?" she asked suspiciously.

"Nowhere in particular. Just a drive."

"You're not hot on the trail of a clue or something?"

He looked disgusted. "No, I'm not hot on the trail of anything. Do you want to take a ride or not?"

"Let me get my purse." During their long trip to reach this place, she couldn't possibly have imagined a ride anywhere as entertainment, but anything looked good today. Dashing to the dresser, she grabbed her purse and returned to the door of her room. "I'm ready."

Tuck led the way through the cabin and made sure the back door was locked behind them. Nicole gratefully inhaled the fresh, damp air. The rain had stopped and a feeble sun was breaking through the clouds. But it felt so good to be outside, she wouldn't have cared if rain was pouring down in sheets.

Settled in the car with Tuck at the wheel, as usual, they drove away. Nicole immediately began to feel better. She was so used to being on the go at home that confinement and immobility felt a lot like being shackled. Though the sun wouldn't be out for long because of the late afternoon hour, it felt wonderful to be driving through some of the most beautiful scenery she'd ever seen.

"Are the winters harsh in this area?" she asked.

"Why? Thinking of moving to Idaho?"

"Well, you have to admit it's a beautiful place."

"Yes, it's beautiful, and yes, the winters are harsh."

"Harsh as in what? Cold temperatures? Snow?"

"Both. Nicole, Coeur d'Alene's only a few hundred miles south of the Canadian line. Maybe not even that far. And you don't get greenery like this without moisture—lots of rain and snow. When I was here before, I talked to a guy who told me that there are years when the lake freezes completely over. He said it hadn't happened in a while, but he remembered when it did. That indicates not just cold temperatures, but long spells of freezing weather."

Nicole sighed. "Well, it's sure pretty in the summer."

"Yeah, and Las Vegas is sure pretty in the winter. Just depends on what you dislike more, cold winters or hot summers. Me, I'll take the hot summers. Never did like snow and ice."

They were just reaching the outskirts of the city when Tuck remembered that he'd left his gun behind. For a moment he was actually stunned. His negligence was going to cut this drive short, he thought with a frown. Now he was getting forgetful? God, would he ever return to normal?

A glance at Nicole put another knot in his gut. An immediate return to the cabin would drop her back into the doldrums. She seemed to be enjoying this outing as though it were something special. For some reason he didn't want to disappoint her.

For some reason he *couldn't* disappoint her.

Uneasily, he drove on into the city.

Six

Concealing his qualms, Tuck said casually, "Let's just drive around and take a look at the town." He didn't want Nicole to suddenly decide to do some shopping, or to get out of the car for any other reason. As long as they stayed in the car, he felt she would be safe.

"Sure, sounds good to me," Nicole agreed.

Slowly they cruised Sherman Avenue, the main downtown thoroughfare. Along with the large hotel complex on the shore of the lake, he spotted numerous motels. He started thinking about that white sports car again. Even if it was in Coeur d'Alene, the odds of spotting it were astronomical. But unless Jillian Marsden knew someone here and was staying in an ordinary residence, she would have to be staying in a motel. Or that impressive hotel, of course.

Nicole was content with studying the shops, restaurants and various businesses they drove past and didn't notice Tuck paying particular attention to the motels. It was such a long shot that Tuck didn't hold much hope for spotting that car, but it gave him something to do while chauffeuring Nicole around the city.

"Coeur d'Alene is much larger than I expected," Nicole commented after Tuck had made a turn onto Fourth Street and it went on for miles before coming into another commercial section of town.

More motels, thought Tuck with a narrowing of his eyes. The town was full of them. Obviously the area's economy relied heavily on tourism.

"It's grown a lot since I was here," he mumbled. He'd never find that white sports car this way. Besides, he had only a gut feeling that Ms. Marsden had even come to Coeur d'Alene, which wasn't much to go on.

The streetlights were starting to come on. Tuck frowned. Along with having no weapon, they would be returning to the cabin in the dark. Damn, where was his mind?

"I think we should be heading back now," he said.

Nicole sighed. "If you say so." She turned slightly to look at Hannigan. "I'd like to say something."

"Go ahead."

"Well...I know I've been a real pain and I'd like to apologize."

"Forget it. You've been under a lot of stress."

"I just wanted you to know that I'll try to do better," Nicole said quietly.

Tuck nodded without looking at her. "Thanks."

Nicole faced front. Hannigan's word of thanks had been almost clipped, certainly unemotional. Not that she'd expected or even hoped for gushing gratitude because of her apology, but must he remain so aloof? Was this his normal personality, or was he so determined to keep them at arm's length because of that kiss that he purposely kept even a trace of warmth from seeping into his voice?

He's a very unusual man, she thought, mulling it over as they started the drive around the lake toward the cabin. That kiss, for example. Any of the men she had dated during the past several years would have interpreted her response to a kiss as permission to go further. Maybe even as a *request* to go further. Not Hannigan. It could be, of course, that he'd acted on impulse and suddenly remembered that he was committed to another woman. And yet he showed no signs of impulsive behavior. He was a man who thought things through, or appeared to be. If that really was the case, why had he kissed her?

He's not only unusual, he's a challenge, Nicole thought, surprising herself with that bizarre assessment. She almost laughed. When had she become a woman intrigued by a challenging man? A man who backed off and guarded his privacy with an armor-plated expression? But then, she hadn't met any of that ilk before, had she? It was she who'd been doing the backing off in Vegas, and maybe that was Hannigan's big draw. With him, she might *not* back off.

She gulped as a flash of heat raced through her body at the provocative picture that idea brought to mind. Hannigan was a handsome guy, and if he ever unbent...

Nicole lowered her window and the damp night air hit her full in the face. It felt great.

"Too warm?" Tuck asked.

"Uh, a little. I'll just leave it down for a minute."

"Leave it down as long as you want, but I could turn on the air conditioner if you'd prefer." He himself wasn't a bit too warm. In fact, with Nicole's window down, the air coming off the water felt chilly.

"No, this is fine."

"You're getting acclimated to cooler weather pretty fast," he remarked. "Maybe you're a Northerner at heart."

"Maybe," Nicole agreed in a weak voice. If he ever caught on that she'd had such personal, erotic thoughts about him, she would die of embarrassment. He was distant and she must follow suit. Anything else from her would only be humiliating for both of them.

But for a fact she was aware of Hannigan as a man, regardless that feelings of a personal nature had no place in their unusual relationship. Staring out the open window into the deepening darkness, she sighed softly, then, after a while, she rolled up the window.

Tuck was thinking about his gun again, lying in the drawer of his bedstand. His negligence in leaving it behind was inexcusable. Neither had he left any lights on in the cabin. They were returning in the dark, which he vowed would never happen again. But self-made promises about future expeditions did nothing to reassure him on this evening's carelessness. The closer they got to the cabin, the tenser he became. Cynicism entered his thoughts. Joe Crawford believed he'd assigned the job of protecting a very important witness to one of his best men; Joe was wrong.

Nicole was surprised when Tuck pulled the car over to the side of the road—so far over it was practically in the ditch—some distance from the cabin's driveway. At the same time he switched off the headlights and engine.

Tuck turned in the seat to peer at her in the dark before she could ask what he was doing. "I want you to wait here until you see lights on in the cabin. That'll be a signal that everything's okay. Then you can drive the car on in."

A frisson of fear darted up Nicole's spine. "Do you think someone's in there?" She squinted in an attempt to see through the trees. The cabin was only slightly visible as a dark, hulking shadow. "We should have left some lights on," she said worriedly.

Yes, and I should have taken my gun with me. Tuck's mouth tightened in self-reproach. He was frightening Nicole, probably without cause, but he couldn't take a chance with her life. He had royally screwed up this evening, starting with his invitation to take a ride with darkness only a few hours away.

He rolled down his window. "Move over here after I get out, and listen. If you hear anything unusual..."

"Unusual?" Nicole's heart was pounding and her throat was dry. "Like what?"

"Just something that shouldn't be there," Tuck said curtly. "If you do, start this car and get the hell away from here. Drive back to town, go to the police station and have someone there call Captain Crawford in Vegas."

"Drive away and...and leave you?"

"Don't worry about me. Just do exactly as I said." Tuck opened his door, got out and then closed the door with the utmost caution, making only a faint clicking noise as the latch caught.

Nicole twisted on the seat to watch him glide around the back of the car, jump the ditch and move into the trees. "My God," she whispered frantically. She didn't like this cloak-and-dagger business one little bit. What made Tuck think it was necessary? Had he seen something, noticed something that had alerted him to danger? Was there someone at the cabin, maybe inside, awaiting their return?

He had his gun, of course, she thought, which alleviated some of her distress. Recalling his instructions then, she scooted over, situating herself behind the wheel. But every cell in her body was clenched and she was afraid to breathe too loudly for fear of missing any sound from outside.

Shivering, she scanned the trees, hoping to catch a glimpse of Hannigan, to no avail. It was as though the night had swallowed him up, as though he had vanished from the face of the earth. Her fearful gaze drifted to the lake, but only momentarily as the dark water and the occasional distant dock or buoy light in that direction merely increased her sensation of being completely alone in an alien land.

Tuck circled the cabin in the trees and approached the building from its hindside. Standing in the shadow of a large pine tree, he studied the scene through sight, sound and smell. Nothing moved. The only sounds came from nocturnal insects. He kept his breathing quiet and felt some relief that he could still move silently when necessary; apparently he hadn't lost *every* instinct he'd once taken for granted.

But this whole damned fiasco was his fault and he'd never forget it. Scaring the hell out of Nicole because of his negligence was unforgivable.

Inhaling slowly, he started toward the cabin, moving with concentrated stealth, using any available shadow as cover. With the same concentration he silently walked around the cabin, checking each window for signs of entry. Everything appeared normal. Reaching the back of the building again, he took out his key and stepped up to the door. With amazing precision, considering how dark it was, he inserted the key into the lock on his first attempt. Opening the door only wide enough to slip inside, he left it ajar a crack and waited a few seconds for his eyes to adjust to the interior blackness. When he could make out the refrigerator and the rest of the kitchen, he began his search of the cabin.

There was nothing amiss. No one was lurking in a closet or behind a door. He started snapping on lamps and ceiling fixtures, until the entire cabin was ablaze with light.

Nicole nearly collapsed with relief. Her hands were trembling, and turning the key in the ignition took monumental effort. Somehow she managed to drive the car into the driveway without mishap. Braking next to the cabin, she turned off the engine and laid her head on the steering wheel, willing her racing heart to calm down.

"Nicole?" Tuck was bent over, peering at her through the open window. "Are you okay?"

Raising her head, she released the tension-laden breath she'd apparently been holding. "Are *you?*"

"Yeah. Everything's fine." He opened the door. "Come on. Get out." He rolled up the window and held out his hand.

Not sure her legs would hold her up, Nicole took it. "What happened? What made you think something was wrong?"

"I'll explain inside." Tuck hung on to her for the short walk to the cabin's door, feeling through physical contact the indisputable proof of her shattered emotions. It had been so damned unnecessary, and he felt like a horse's rump for putting her through this.

Inside in the light he saw the strung-out pallor of her skin. He led her to the living room and a chair. "Sit down." She sank into the chair like a deflating balloon, all limp and lifeless. "I'll get you something to drink. Don't move."

Moving wasn't on her agenda. Now that the crisis had passed, whatever it had been, she was feeling the debilitating aftermath of overwhelming fright and tension. Her head fell back against the chair, seemingly too heavy for her neck to support.

Tuck opened cupboards in the kitchen, looking for the three bottles of dinner wine Nicole had picked out the day they'd shopped for groceries. He wished now that he'd included a bottle of brandy in their order, though at the time it hadn't entered his mind that they might actually need something stronger than wine. He didn't need it, but Nicole did. A shot of brandy would arrest the shock she was still feeling and put color back into her face.

Finally locating the wine, Tuck took down a bottle of cabernet, deciding it would have to do. Uncorking the bottle, he poured a water glass about half full and carried it back to the living room.

He held it out. "Here, drink this."

Nicole's eyes fluttered open. "Wine?"

"You need it. Take it. I wish it were brandy or whiskey."

She really didn't have the strength to refuse, and maybe a few sips of wine would help her get her bearings, she rationalized while weakly lifting her hand to accept the glass.

Tuck lowered himself to a chair, leaned forward in it, and watched her take a swallow, then another. A strange mixture of emotions and feelings gathered within him—remorse for his carelessness, self-directed anger for the same reason, empathy for Nicole and her situation, and an almost intolerable need to go to her, to hold and comfort her, to assure her that nothing like tonight would ever happen again.

Her eyes met his and she spoke in a voice that sounded frayed and unsteady. "I've never been so frightened in my life. What happened?"

He suddenly didn't want to appear inept in her eyes, which was damned odd when he couldn't have cared less what she thought of him before tonight.

He lied. "I didn't know you'd get so scared over ordinary police procedure."

"Tonight was ordinary?" There was skepticism and outright astonishment in her eyes. "You mean that you live your life creeping around in the dark night after night? How do you bear a job like that?"

"It's not like that. Believe it or not, just as many arrests are made in broad daylight as occur after dark." It was a vague variation of the truth. Some crimes were more prevalent during daylight hours, some after dark. Banks, for instance, were held up during the day because they were only open during the day. Murders were committed at any hour. Family disturbances occurred at any hour, although holidays were notorious for bringing out the worst in families. People drove drunk at any hour, though most of the arrests in that category took place at night.

"Do you actually *like* being a cop?" Along with the skepticism and astonishment in Nicole's eyes, Tuck saw incredulity. He'd run into her attitude before. People who weren't in law enforcement had a hard time understanding why anyone would choose risking life and limb on a daily basis for a career.

Tuck didn't answer right away. Her question had hit him in a very tender spot. He *had* liked being a cop, but that was before he'd killed two men. The gist of Nicole's query was what he'd been trying to figure out ever since.

"It's a job," he finally said offhandedly.

For a few minutes Hannigan had been as human as herself, Nicole realized, but right before her eyes he'd returned to that distant place in which he kept himself separate from the rest of humanity. Pity the woman who fell in love with Tuck Hannigan, she thought.

Since he was no longer compassionate and polite, she saw no reason for her to hold anything back. "I'm not completely convinced tonight was merely ordinary police procedure," she said, daring him with a look to challenge her statement. "I think there's something you're not telling me."

Tuck got to his feet. "Think what you want. If you're feeling all right now, I'm going to bed."

Nicole finished the last of the wine in the glass. "I may never be all right again, but I'm sure you won't lose any sleep over it. Good night."

Tuck started from the room. "When you go to bed, turn off all of the inside lights. Leave the outside ones on. I've already seen to locking the doors."

"Your every word is my command," she drawled.

Ignoring her sarcasm, Tuck continued on to his bedroom. He undressed and got into bed, but his hope of falling asleep was almost laughable. Remnants of the tension he'd undergone during the past hour still held his body rigid. He told himself that checking the cabin before letting Nicole come in had only been sensible. But the fact remained that if he'd done his job right in the first place, it could have all been handled without scaring her witless.

He was too easily spooked now, he thought with a discomfiting sensation in his gut. He never should have taken this job. Damn Joe for talking him into it, and damn himself for letting Joe's cushy-job routine influence his judgment. He should be alone somewhere, sorting things through, trying to understand who he was now. If Nicole got hurt because of his incompetence . . .

The thought was too abhorrent to complete. What Joe had said about her being a nice woman was true. What Joe *hadn't* said was another truth: she was strikingly attractive, sexy in an understated, disturbingly feminine way. At least, she was disturbing Tuck. He was noticing his own reactions to her movements, her voice, her scent, more and more. Maybe awareness of her physical charms was only natural, given the circumstances. Put a man and a woman in the same small space for any length of time and something was bound to happen, either intense dislike or intense desire. In his and Nicole's case, Tuck feared it was going to be the latter.

He thought of that kiss and her response, and felt a rush of blood to his groin. Groaning, he turned over, punched his pillow into another configuration and forced his eyes to shut. It wasn't going to happen, dammit. It simply was not going to happen. He wouldn't let it. Making love to the woman he was duty-bound to protect would be the act of a damned fool. He might be different than he'd been before those shootings, but he hadn't yet reached the fool-for-a-day stage.

After Tuck's abrupt departure, Nicole got up, went to the kitchen and poured herself some more wine. The trembling of her hands and the weakness in her legs had passed, thank goodness. The wine had helped, obviously, even if it had also made her head feel a little woozy. But wooziness was a whole lot better than fear. God, she'd never been so scared in her entire life. And for what? Because of "ordinary police procedure"? Bull! Did Hannigan think her a complete idiot? Something had occurred that she had missed and Tuck hadn't. Had he seen a face from Vegas during their drive? He'd seen something, but what? Why wouldn't he tell her about it? Why clam up the way he had?

Switching off the kitchen light, Nicole returned to the living room. Before resuming her seat, she turned off all of the lights except for the small lamp next to her chair. She wasn't sleepy, and in fact was too keyed-up to even lie down. The wine was good, and each swallow seemed to relax her a bit more.

Now that her fear had dissipated, questions about Hannigan's "ordinary police procedure" kept stacking up in her mind. For one, if they were out after dark again, would he put her through the same frightening exercise as tonight? If only he would explain. Why *wouldn't* he explain? It was frustrating to be ignorant of something that plainly revolved around her.

God knew her questions weren't because she thought him incompetent. If anything, Hannigan went too far the other way. He was going to protect her if he smothered the breath out of her doing it.

Sighing, Nicole finished her wine, got up and took the empty glass to the kitchen sink. With a shower in mind, she switched off the little lamp in the living room and made her way in the dark down the hall to her bedroom.

The shower felt wonderful. Turning her face up to the spray, Nicole realized that her system had returned to normal. She was relaxed now and even a little sleepy. Good. When she got into bed, she wouldn't roll and toss from anxiety.

Turning the water off, she stepped out of the stall and reached for a towel. Her hand froze at the sudden, sharp cracking noise from outside, as though someone had stepped on a dry limb that had fallen from one of the trees.

Fear immediately constricted her throat and for several moments she couldn't move. But then mobility returned in a rush and she hastily snapped off the overhead light. Grabbing the towel, she wrapped it around herself, darted into her bedroom, where she extinguished those lights, and then ran down the hall to Hannigan's door.

"Tuck?" she whispered. No answer. "Hannigan?" Still no response.

With her heart pounding, she turned the knob and pushed open his door. He heard her at the same time she saw him in bed, and he bounded up, grabbing the gun he'd placed on his nightstand.

"It's me!" Nicole cried, aware of that awful weapon pointed at her.

Tuck squinted in the dark, recognized Nicole and realized she was only wearing a towel. He lowered the gun. "What's going on?"

"I heard a noise...just outside my bathroom." Her voice was shaking. Her wet hair was drizzling water down her neck to her bare shoulders. "I was just getting out of the shower when I heard it."

Tuck was already off the bed. Without stopping for clothes, he walked past Nicole in his briefs. "Stay right behind me," he whispered.

She wouldn't be anywhere else, she thought with a shudder. Not on a dare. If it were possible, she would glue herself to his back. Behind him she felt safe from whatever was lurking outside in the dark.

Moving quietly, Tuck entered first Nicole's bedroom and then her bathroom, aware of her all but breathing down his neck. She had taken his instructions literally and couldn't be more than two inches from his back.

Her bathroom was still steamy from her shower. Cautiously, Tuck separated two slats in the miniblind at the one tiny window to peer out. Then he grinned. Outside was a fat little porcupine, sniffing and shuffling through brush and twigs.

Tuck turned slightly—he had very little space with Nicole standing so close. "Take a look."

"Outside?" Her wide, frightened eyes registered surprise.

"It's a porcupine. Check it out for yourself."

"A porcupine!"

Tuck rolled up the blind and they exchanged places, with Nicole ducking under Tuck's arm to see out and him standing behind her to look over the top of her head.

"Well, I'll be..." Nicole mumbled. "I've never seen a porcupine in his natural habitat before. What's he doing?"

"Probably feeding."

"He gave me a few gray hairs, I can tell you." She turned around. "Tuck, I'm sorry I woke you. I guess I'm just jumpy because of..." Her voice trailed off as it occurred to her that they were mere inches apart, him in his underwear, her wearing a towel. His white briefs appeared almost luminous against the darker tones of his skin and she wondered if her white towel looked the same to him.

"You didn't wake me. I hadn't fallen asleep yet." Even he noticed the husky timbre of his voice. The setting, though a little bizarre, bore an intimate quality and he was feeling it in the pit of his stomach. Nicole was shadowy and looked mysteriously beautiful, and the air was redolent with the scents of soap and shampoo. "Besides," he added in an even hoarser voice, "feel free to wake me anytime. It's what I'm here for."

Nicole swallowed. He wasn't dashing away. That he was seemingly rooted to the spot and immersed in the situation—her own feelings exactly—made her pulse race and her heart beat in an erratic pattern. She could like this man, she thought within the euphoric daze of her mind. With any encouragement at all, she could *really* like him. Unquestionably there was chemistry simmering between them. One move from either of them right now would have them in each other's arms.

Tuck was thinking virtually the same thoughts, but he was also at war with himself. Touch her now—he sensed she wouldn't object—and their relationship would change forever. He'd rued that other kiss the second it was over, and he had a feeling that in this steamy little bathroom in the dark, a kiss would merely be a prelude to much deeper involvement.

His gun was still in his hand. It was as good an excuse as any to break up this unexpected tête-à-tête. Backing up a step, he raised the gun slightly, just so she would see it.

"I'm going to put this away," he mumbled thickly. Then he got the hell out of there before he changed his mind and did something that he *knew* he'd regret in the morning.

Nicole stared at the vacant doorway with her mouth open. He couldn't have retreated any faster. "You . . . you coward,'' she whispered, shaken by the intensity of the disappointment rattling around in her system. He'd felt exactly what she had, she would bet anything she possessed on it, only he'd denied it and fled.

Challenging, definitely. Nicole's eyes narrowed in speculation. Just how noble was Tuck Hannigan?

Wouldn't it be interesting to find out?

Seven

After a nearly silent breakfast, Nicole began tidying the kitchen and Tuck went outside. She rinsed the dishes and placed them in the dishwasher, frowning all the while. They were more uncomfortable with each other than they'd ever been, obviously because of those few moments in the bathroom last night when more than a porcupine had been on their minds.

Nicole was still fussing with this and that, folding a dish towel, hanging it on a rack, wiping counters, when she heard sharp, hacking noises from outside. They sounded like an ax in use, but why would Hannigan be chopping wood? The sun was bright again. They certainly didn't need a fire. In fact, even during yesterday's rainstorm and Tuck's mentioning he liked wood fires, he hadn't started one.

Nicole went to the window to see what was really happening. Exactly as she'd suspected, Tuck was wielding an ax and whacking the hell out of chunks of wood, chopping them into small pieces, apparently slated for the fireplace or, on second thought, to add to that pile of *already* chopped wood next to the small storage shed that was partially hidden in the trees.

It was a beautiful day and Nicole had no intention of staying inside herself. Almost belligerently she went through the back door and folded her arms. "*Why* are you chopping wood?"

Tossing two pieces of split wood to the ground near the chopping block, he gave her a disgruntled look. "For something to do."

Her sigh sounded like a complaint. "I need something to do, too. Do you have any objections to my walking down to the lake?"

Tuck laid down the ax. "I'll go with you."

"That isn't necessary," she said. "I'm not afraid of porcupines."

He shot her an unamused look. "Come on. If you want to go down to the lake, we'll go to the lake."

He took off walking around the cabin and headed down the slope toward the water. Although she followed, this wasn't what Nicole had had in mind. She would just as soon be alone. In fact, she preferred being alone. After last night she wasn't quite sure how she felt about Hannigan. Thinking of him as a challenge was not only foreign to her nature, it seemed foolish this morning.

Tuck parked himself on a rock. There were several around, good-sized, scattered along the beach. Nicole picked up a few pebbles, tossed them into the water, then dipped her hand in. She glanced back at Tuck.

"The water's really quite warm. Do you think it's safe to swim along here?"

"Do you want to go swimming?"

She shrugged. "It's a thought. I can't just do nothing day after day. Yesterday was intolerable. You thought so, too. Locked in the cabin just because it was raining. The rain wasn't your fault, of course, but neither was it mine."

"No, it was no one's fault. Take a swim if you want. Looks pretty safe. I can see the bottom for quite a ways out there. Just don't go out too far."

"I'm a good swimmer," Nicole said tartly. "You really do worry about me a little too much, don't you think?"

His expression was cool and unreadable. "That's what I'm being paid for."

She straightened from the water's edge. "Are you being paid a lot for this job?"

"Standard pay," he said. "Nothing to get excited about."

She put her hands on her hips. "Were you ordered to take this job, or did you volunteer?"

He laughed, a sharp, staccato sound. "I sure as hell didn't volunteer."

"Then you were ordered."

"No, I wasn't ordered, either. I asked for some time off— my vacation time and sick leave. It added up to about six weeks. I wanted to get away from Vegas. Captain Crawford suggested that if I wanted to just get out of Vegas for a while, I might be interested in this job. I thought it over for a few minutes—it was all he gave me to think about it—and I said okay. What he didn't tell me and I didn't think to ask was who the person was that I would be protecting."

"Meaning?"

"Meaning I didn't know the witness was a woman."

"Ah. And when you found out the witness was female, you didn't like it."

"Not particularly," he replied.

She felt for the first time that she was seeing beneath the hard exterior of Hannigan's demeanor. He'd wanted time off, been talked into taking this job, found out that he would be protecting a woman and hadn't liked it. Consequently, before he'd ever met her he hadn't liked her.

She waited a few seconds, not quite glaring at him but certainly not laying a pleasant look on him, and finally said, "I'm going to go change into my suit. I don't suppose *you'd* care to go swimming."

"No," he said flatly. "I'll just sit here and watch you swim."

From his tone he obviously thought she wasn't much of a swimmer. She sniffed. "I'm probably a better swimmer than you are."

"You might be better than I am at a lot of things," he said in a voice that implied, *So what?*

Nicole went up the hill toward the cabin. Tuck reached down, picked up some small rocks and gave them a fierce toss into the water. He didn't like this whole setup, starting with what had nearly happened in Nicole's bathroom last night.

What's more, he didn't like *anyone* knowing where they were. Despite Joe's confidence that only some top people in the department were aware, or would be made aware, of what was going on, there were always leaks. Secretaries talked and cops speculated about rumors among themselves. He'd been on the force long enough to know that in-house secrets were damned hard to keep.

For one thing, the prosecutor's office knew about there being a reliable witness, and there were numerous people working in the prosecutor's office. Whether they were all trustworthy or not was a damned good question.

Joe had told him not to call again without good reason, but he wanted to talk to Joe. He wanted to ask him, "Is there a possibility of a leak?" He also wanted to find out for himself if he was being overly protective and spooked without a reason. Of course, he wouldn't ask Joe *those* questions; asking them of himself was bad enough.

Nicole came down the hill wearing a royal blue cover-up that stopped at her upper thighs. Her legs were bare, lightly tanned and beautiful. Tuck didn't miss them. Without looking his way, she discarded the cover-up and stood for a moment in a matching blue bathing suit before wading into the water.

Now here was something he *did* like—the way she looked in a bathing suit—which wasn't especially comforting. She was slender, with narrow hips and nicely rounded breasts, the type of woman he was normally drawn to. She ducked into the water and began swimming. She'd told him the truth: she was a good swimmer. Her overhand crawl was smooth and appeared effortless. Tuck never took his eyes off her.

She turned over on her back, floated and called, "It's really great. Why don't you get your bathing suit and come in?"

He felt the urge to do so, to join her in the water, to let go and have some fun. It had been a long time since he'd had fun, this kind of fun. But something held him back, probably the memory of last night and how close he'd come to making a bad mistake.

The sound of a speedboat jerked Tuck's eyes in its direction. There were so many boats on the lake that he wasn't immediately alarmed. But the boat seemed aimed at Nicole, and it kept coming. It was still some distance away when he jumped up. "Nicole! Get out of the water!"

"What?" she called.

He waded in, shoes and all. "Get out of the water. Do it now, fast!"

She looked at him as though he'd lost his mind. But then she heard the boat and she turned in the water to see it coming toward her. Surely it would veer, she thought, but maybe the driver didn't see her. She started swimming toward land. When her feet could touch bottom, Tuck was there to grab her by the arm and haul her to shore. The boat sped past, a white craft trimmed in blue. The driver was covered up, wearing an oversize T-shirt and a hat. There was no one else in the boat.

Tuck cursed under his breath. Was *this* his imagination? Had the boat been aimed at Nicole? If so, someone was keeping very close tabs on their activities. A neighbor, someone farther away with field glasses?

He kept hold of her arm and dragged her away from the water. She shook off his hand and picked up her cover-up with a scowl. "That boat really wasn't going to hit me."

"Oh, you know that?" he said somewhat sarcastically.

"Well, it certainly wasn't going to hit me on purpose!"

He didn't argue with her. He merely said, "I think you've swam enough for today."

She sighed in frustration. "Well, let's go lock ourselves in the cabin. Then nothing can get to me, can it?"

"You know, you're taking this pretty damned lightly," he said harshly. "This whole thing."

"And you're taking it too damned seriously," she snapped. "No one knows we're here. No one knows *I'm* here, and yet you see danger and a threat to me in every occurrence. I still don't understand what happened last night, why I had to wait in the car while you checked the cabin, and I'm sure I never will because you don't talk."

"Don't be ridiculous. I talk just as much as anyone else."

"Oh, give me a break, Hannigan. You say only the bare minimum."

Their retreat to the cabin was conducted in sullen silence. Nicole's system reeked with resentment, resentment of Hannigan's excessive protectiveness, of Joe Crawford, who'd apparently planned this whole awful fiasco, of the other detectives who'd scared her away from windows, resentment of herself because she'd been stupid enough to make that telephone call reporting what she'd seen, resentment because she was probably going to lose her job over this miserable affair, and maybe the hardest to deal with, resentment because in spite of everything else, Hannigan made her feel like a woman.

But he was about as romantic as a rock, and why she'd been putting him and romance in the same thought was an unnerving mystery, one she had absolutely no hope of solving.

Entering the cabin, she went directly to her bedroom.

After Nicole showered away the lake water, she donned a robe and lay on her bed. Her mind was full, her thoughts jumping around like popcorn in a skillet. What was happening in Las Vegas? Thinking of her job and what might be going on in the Monte Carlo's purchasing department was unbearably frustrating, so she forced that topic aside to question what, if any, headway the police department and prosecutor's office were making in the Buckley murder case. Was it asking too much to be kept informed? Wasn't she entitled to hear of any progress, however small?

Sliding off the bed, she tightened the sash of her robe while leaving her room to ask Hannigan those questions. She found him in the kitchen, seated at the table and hunched over a mug of coffee.

He'd been brooding over that boat, one minute telling himself the incident had been accidental and the next, certain it wasn't.

He looked up to see Nicole's frigid expression. "I don't want to hear it," he said gruffly.

"Hear what?" she retorted. "You don't know what's on my mind."

"Like hell I don't. You're ticked off because I ordered you out of the water."

"Your giving orders is old hat, Hannigan. That's *not* why I'm in here talking to you. I want to know if Crawford and his people have made any progress in Vegas. Call him and find out."

Tuck sat back. "He said he'd do the calling. When there was something we should know."

"That's not good enough! Doesn't he realize that even the smallest gain would give me some relief? Call him, or I will."

"Sorry, but I can't let you do that."

Their gazes locked in a stare down while Nicole's anger grew. He wasn't going to let her call anyone. She felt so trapped that she wanted to scream.

Instead her lip curled. "You're sorry? I'll just bet you are." Whirling, she flounced from the kitchen and returned to her bedroom, cursing Hannigan every step of the way.

She flopped onto the bed again. Hannigan wasn't just her bodyguard, he was her captor, damn him!

That boat hadn't been trying to run over her. Good Lord, boats raced by all the time. Hadn't they both watched one speed past just the other evening? It was probably the same boat, the same driver, some idiot who disregarded safety and made a habit of coming too close to shore.

The bottom line, which Hannigan couldn't seem to get through his thick skull, was that no one knew she was here. She just couldn't believe that someone had managed to follow their circuitous route from Las Vegas to northern Idaho. By the same token, Hannigan seemed so in control, certainly not an alarmist. The truth was, she didn't know what to believe.

A second truth was that she wasn't feeling particularly safe here and she didn't know what she should do about it, if there was anything she *could* do about it. Not when he wouldn't even let her use the telephone. Taking off on her own, going somewhere all by herself, hiding out, was a horrifying thought. How had she ever come to this, a person like her? She'd always abided by the law, lived by the law.

She grimaced. That was how she'd gotten into this fix, doing her lawful duty. She *had* to rely on Hannigan's judgment, irritating as it was. What else could she do? And he'd only been playing it safe by pulling her out of the water. She shouldn't be an alarmist, either.

Up and pacing the main room of the cabin, Tuck was having similar thoughts. His, however, were tinged with uneasy questions about himself, really only a repeat of the same questions that had been badgering him since the convenience-store shootings, all of them revolving around his reactions, judgments and instincts. He hadn't expected to be playing detective during this job and that was what he was doing, suspecting everyone and every incident. Was he right, wrong, or somewhere in between?

Like Nicole, he felt the urge to call Joe Crawford. *Were* they making any headway in Vegas, proving that Spencer had been with Lowicki that night? He was still mulling it all over, worrying about it, looking at it from all angles, when Nicole walked in. She was dressed in yellow shorts and a white blouse, and her expression was not friendly.

"I want to go to town," she said without preamble.

He regarded her with a questioning and unblinking look. "What for?"

"I need to pick up a few things, some personal items."

He thought about it. He didn't want to take her to town but he certainly couldn't let her go by herself; he couldn't keep her locked up in this cabin indefinitely; and he didn't want her swimming in the lake anymore. His nerves were raw and jagged, and maybe without any good reason. In his own way he was as confused as Nicole, and he didn't like the feeling.

He finally conceded to her wishes simply because he was tired of saying no. "All right, we'll go to town."

This time he left lights on even though it was still early in the day, just in case something kept them away until after dark, made sure the doors were locked, and took his gun, playing it as safely as he knew how.

They got in the car. "Thank you," Nicole said stiffly.

He didn't answer. They drove the winding road around the lake to the city that was becoming more familiar with each trip. He drove directly to a large shopping center, which contained one of those huge drug complexes that should carry any personal item a woman could possibly need.

He pulled into a parking slot. "You don't need to come in with me," Nicole said. "I'm perfectly capable of doing a little shopping on my own."

Tuck was tired of arguing the same points with her, over and over again. Saying nothing, he got out of the car, locked it, and followed her into the drugstore.

She tried to ignore him as he trailed her up one aisle and down another. She picked up some shampoo and toothpaste, and some things she didn't need, like a bottle of nail polish and a lipstick. She fussed around in the cosmetic department for a while and finally said, "Okay, I'll go check out now."

He'd tried not to let his impatience show, but hanging around the cosmetic department of any store was definitely not a favorite pastime of his. Relieved that she was through with her shopping, he followed her to the checkout stand.

It wasn't long before they were in the car again. Nicole tossed her package into the back seat and fastened her seat belt. With a sidelong glance at Hannigan, she said, "Let's not go back to the cabin yet. Please."

He heard the plea in her voice. If his nerves were raw and jagged, so were hers. Before starting the car, he turned his head and looked at her, and felt that sympathetic tug again. Only this time it was accompanied by personal feelings that were developing regardless of his private arguments against any such thing. He didn't want to get involved with Nicole Currie, and yet it was happening. Not just because she was a pretty woman. Not because she was a woman in trouble. There was something connecting them, something he didn't have a lot of experience with, something that was felt, not seen or heard or tangible in any way. Just something that was felt, deep inside of him.

"Nicole," he said. "I don't want anything to happen to you."

She looked slightly surprised. "I believe that. I think you're doing everything you can. In fact, as I told you before, you're probably doing too much. I—I feel smothered."

"Yes, I'm sure you do. It's going to get worse before it gets better, Nicole."

"How can it?" she asked with a heavy sigh.

"Any way you look at it, we've only gotten started. It took a couple of days to get here, we've only been here a few days so far, and it could go on for weeks. They told you that in Vegas."

"Yes, they did," she said. "But I think that something like this isn't something you can visualize when you've had all the freedom in the world. Until recently I've never been afraid of anything. I don't live my life in fear, and that's what I've had to do ever since I made that call."

"I know," he said quietly. "I'm really sorry about that."

"Is this what happens to everyone who reports a crime, or the possibility of a crime?" she asked.

"No. No, of course not. This is unusual. Most witnesses or people who call in...they're in no danger whatsoever. It's handled through the secret witness program, and their name doesn't even have to be known. But in your case, this whole thing is different because they want to put away Spencer as well as Lowicki. That was explained to you, wasn't it?"

"Yes," she said with a sigh. "It was explained to me. Repeatedly." She looked out the window. The parking lot was crowded; it was a busy shopping center. "I still don't want to go back to the cabin. Not yet. Please."

He couldn't say no, not when she sounded so forlorn. "Okay. We'll take a ride."

"Another ride," she said, disappointed. "There must be something to do. This is a tourist town. You can see it everywhere you look. There are restaurants, shopping, swimming, boating, golf. Look at all the people."

"I know, Nicole, I know. And while we're supposed to appear to be a couple on vacation, we're not a couple on vacation. Those are things people do on vacation. We are not on vacation." There was a note of impatience in his voice, reinforced by the way he had repeated himself.

"Fine," she said. "Fine. Just drive somewhere, then. I don't care where."

He started the car, put it in gear, backed out of the parking slot and started driving toward the street.

"Wait a minute," Nicole cried.

He slammed on the brakes. "What?"

"There's a bakery right there. See it?"

He saw where she was pointing. "I see it."

"Let me run in and buy something good, something sweet."

His patience was getting very thin, and he had an awful knot of apprehension in his gut to deal with, as well. Damn! Was he going to live on the edge for the rest of his life? But he couldn't shed the feeling that they shouldn't be there.

Though his lips were pinched from stress, he nodded. "I'll pull up in front of the bakery, you run in and get what you want and come right back out." The bakery was one of the smaller businesses in the massive shopping center and he figured he could wait out front, she could run in, and he would be able to see her every second of the time.

He did as he'd said; drove over to the bakery, stopped right in front and parked in a No Parking area. She wasn't in there more than two minutes when along came a security guard. He tapped on Tuck's window. "Sir, you can't park here. Move along, please."

Tuck glanced into the bakery shop, saw Nicole standing in front of a glass case, obviously deciding what she wanted, and he rolled down his window. "Just a few minutes, sir? My wife is in the bakery. She won't be long."

"No, sorry, but this is a fire lane, mister. We have to follow the directives of the fire department, and there's no parking permitted along here. There's a space right over there, sir. Look over there."

Tuck saw the space to which the guard was referring. It wasn't very far away, so he nodded. "Okay, fine. I'll move." He drove to the parking space with the intention of jumping out and running over to the bakery to escort Nicole back to the car.

She came out from the bakery and looked around. Tuck tooted the horn to catch her attention, but his horn wasn't the only one tooting and she kept looking for him. All of a sudden she spotted him. He was getting out of the car and he waved at her, telling her by gesture to wait there, that he would walk over to her and then walk her back to the car.

Or, now that she was outside, he could drive over and pick her up. That made more sense. He got back into the car, started it and had just begun backing out of the parking space when he noticed Nicole starting across the road, the fire lane, according to the security guard.

A black van appeared out of nowhere. Tuck caught it out of the corner of his eye. He saw it speeding toward Nicole. The security guard, who hadn't gotten very far away, also saw it, and seemed to freeze in his tracks. Nicole, apparently, was the only one who didn't see it.

Sweat broke out on Tuck's body. That boat hadn't been an accident, and neither was this. Lowicki and Spencer knew Nicole was in Coeur d'Alene and this was another attempt on her life!

Tuck jumped out of the car and started running. Somehow, God only knew how, he rushed in front of the van and pushed Nicole to the sidewalk. The van sped on past.

She had skinned knees. The breath was knocked out of her. The palms of her hands were stinging, and the cookies she had purchased were scattered all over the sidewalk. The security guard came running over. Other people began gathering.

Tuck tried to get the license number of the van and saw that the plate was smeared with mud. But it was a black van with darkly tinted windows, and the one thing he knew for sure was that it was driven by a person with long red hair, possibly a wig. He put that out of his mind for the moment. The van was gone. There was nothing he could do about it.

He turned to Nicole. "Are you all right?"

"No, I'm not all right," she said angrily. "I'm hurt, I'm confused. What in hell is going on?"

The security guard interrupted. "Ma'am, are you all right?" Nicole just looked at him without answering. "I'm going to call the police," the man said.

Tuck looked up at him. "Do whatever you think is right, man."

As soon as the guard hurried away, Tuck said to Nicole, "Come on. Let's get the hell out of here." He pulled her to her feet, dragged her over to the car, which was still running, put her in the front seat, and drove away.

Nicole started crying, sobbing quietly. "That van tried to run me down, didn't it?"

Tuck's lips were in a thin, grim line. "Yes."

"And so did the boat."

"I think so, yes."

"They know I'm here."

"In my opinion, yes." It was a relief to have faith in his own opinion again. In fact, he felt like a burden had suddenly vanished. He knew how to protect Nicole, only he couldn't do it here. After a moment he said, "We're going back to the cabin. I need to make a phone call. While I'm on the phone, I want you to start packing your things."

"Pack! Where are we going now?"

"I don't know, but we are leaving. Somehow they followed us to Coeur d'Alene. If they didn't follow us, Nicole, there's been a leak in the department in Vegas and Lowicki knows where you are. There's someone here, someone they either knew to contact or sent from Vegas, and I'm not going to gloss it over for you anymore. You're in grave danger."

His features were rigid with determination. "But at least I know what to do about it now." One thing was in his favor: whoever was trying to shut Nicole's mouth for good had been given instructions to make it look like an accident. That was the reason there'd been no gunplay, why no one had invaded the cabin.

Yeah, he knew exactly what he had to do now.

Eight

Nicole was crumpled in the corner of the seat, almost against the door. "Hook your seat belt," Tuck told her. Her hands were trembling, but she managed to latch the belt. Then she dug in her purse for tissues, wiped her eyes, blew her nose and shook with debilitating fear. Her life was in jeopardy. She was in *grave danger*, Hannigan's own words.

Maybe she hadn't really believed it before, though certainly she'd been told how far Lowicki and Spencer would go to keep themselves out of prison. Detective John Harper had presented the situation in kindly terms, however, warning her without any ghoulish details. He should have been more explicit, she thought while sopping up another onslaught of tears. He should have said, "They'll use any weapon to get rid of you, Nicole, so watch out for cars. And boats."

It was suddenly too much. "I can't go on like this," she sobbed.

Tuck drove with one hand and reached out to her with the

other, laying it on her shoulder. "You won't have to. You have my word."

His hand on her shoulder and empathetic tone of voice startled the tears from her eyes. But then she remembered how uncooperative she'd been, balking at his every order, and her eyes filled again. There'd been no real need to go to town today. She'd been resentful, bored and obstinate, and had decided to push him just as hard as he'd been pushing her.

Well, her adolescent rebellion had almost gotten her killed. Groaning out loud, she held a handful of tissues to her eyes.

"Take it easy," Tuck said quietly.

"I've been such a damned fool," she said bitterly. "You've not only had to watch out for me, you've had to put up with my bad humor."

He couldn't disagree, and they drove the rest of the way to the cabin in silence. Tuck parked as close to the back door as he could fit the car. Not close enough, in his estimation, but it would have to do.

Inside, he went directly to the phone. "Start packing," he told her when she stood by with a downcast expression.

"All right, but first I have to ask you something. How did the driver of that van know we were in town? How did the driver of the boat know I was swimming? People are watching us, aren't they?"

He'd been hoping she wouldn't figure that out. He drew a breath. "Yes, I believe they are."

"Then how are we going to drive away without being seen? They'll follow us again. Wherever we go, won't the same thing happen?"

He picked up the phone. "Trust me, Nicole. I know what I'm doing."

"I...trust you," she whispered, and stumbled out of the room.

Placing the phone back onto the receiver, Tuck stared after her. Just knowing they had to leave this place wasn't enough; he had to come up with a feasible way of doing it.

But what worried him now was that the animals trying to kill Nicole and make it appear accidental had tipped their hand today. They had failed at two different attempts, and they had to know that the cop guarding her was on to them.

Tuck frowned. Did they know the cop's name, as well? He'd had a run-in with Nick Lowicki a few years back, having busted that lowlife on a drug charge. Lowicki had gotten off on a technicality, but Tuck would bet anything Lowicki remembered him.

More important, though, now that Nicole's stalkers had given themselves away, would they forget about "accidental" and come after her with a weapon? Tuck scowled. The cabin's doors and windows were all locked, but it would take him about two minutes to break into the place if he were so inclined; he couldn't discount the assassin's ability to do the same.

Getting to his feet, he went to one of the drapery-covered windows and moved the fabric aside just enough to see out. Someone was watching them, but from where? Behind the cabin was a forest of trees, the road, and then a sharply ascending, heavily treed mountain. Someone could be perched up there on that mountain, but with such a density of trees and brush, he wouldn't have an unobstructed view. It seemed more sensible to think that they were being watched from the front of the cabin, which meant the lake.

Tuck studied the scene. Boats and water skiers crisscrossed the water; only what he'd come to expect on a sunny day. His gaze went farther out and lit on a beautiful white cabin cruiser. His pulse began a faster beat. He'd seen and admired that cruiser before. It appeared to be anchored. With high-powered glasses, a person on that craft could see everything that occurred on shore.

That's where they are, Tuck thought with a sudden instinctual conviction, out there on that beautiful boat. From there they had seen Nicole appear in her bathing suit and wade into the water. From there they had issued hasty instructions to a person in the speed boat. From there they had seen them get in the car and head for the city. The driver of the van must wait in town for his or her instructions.

So...how many lowlifes was he dealing with? Tuck wondered with an angry twist to his lips. Two? Five? A dozen?

"Damn right there's a leak," he muttered as he dropped the drapery back into place and returned to the phone. Sitting in the chair, he dialed Captain Crawford's private number.

It rang five times before it was answered. "Hello?"

"Joe, this is Tuck."

"Uh, hello. I can't talk right now. I'm in the middle of a meeting."

"You don't have to talk. Just listen. Lowicki knows where we are. There've been two attempts on the lady's life and we're getting the hell out of here. I don't know where we'll end up, but I'll call in periodically. You can hang up now, if you want."

"Let me call you back. Shouldn't be more than a half hour."

"I can't guarantee we'll still be here, but do what you want. Incidentally, there's been nothing 'cushy' about this job," Tuck added with heavy sarcasm.

"There should have been."

Joe's voice sounded normal. He was probably doing a hell of an acting job for whomever was in his office for that meeting, maintaining an impassive expression and speaking into the phone as though the subject matter was of small import. But Tuck knew Joe well enough to hear the tension behind the normalcy.

Tuck's own tension relented a little. Maybe he'd been blaming Joe for this mess, he thought, which wasn't fair to the older man. "Go ahead and call, Joe. We'll still be here in a half hour. Talk to you later." He hung up.

His thoughts immediately returned to that cruiser in the middle of the lake. Rising, he went to peek through the draperies and wasn't a bit surprised that it was still there. The sixty-four-dollar question was, did the dirtbags watching the cabin have the kind of sophisticated infrared equipment that would enable them to see so far away after dark? Even if they did, darkness was still a good cover. So were the trees between the water's edge and the cabin.

Tuck had the uneasy feeling that everyone involved in this mess was waiting for dark. After today's aborted attempts on Nicole's life, the thugs had to move in quickly. Tonight would be it, Tuck was positive.

Strangely, he was mentally prepared for a sudden attack, though he really didn't expect any trouble until nightfall. He checked his gun, which was standard issue for Metro officers, a Smith & Wesson, containing fifteen rounds. It was loaded and ready for action.

The phone rang. Tuck quickly left the window to answer it. "Hello?"

"I cut the meeting short, Tuck. What in hell's going on?"

Tuck sat down. "There had to be a leak in Vegas, either deliberate or unintentional, Joe. From where I stand it doesn't matter how the information got out, but it sure as hell means something on your end. And I'll tell you something else. I feel pretty damned certain that it occurred before Nicole and I ever left Vegas. Lowicki's people have known every move we've made. Right now there's a cabin cruiser anchored offshore. I don't know how wide the lake is in miles, but the ship looks to be about half to three-quarters of a mile away. I've noticed it before without suspecting its purpose."

"You said there were two attempts on Nicole's life."

"There were. One with a speedboat while she was swimming just offshore and the other in town when a black van tried to run her down at a shopping center."

Joe mumbled a curse. "Tuck, listen to me. I think you're wrong about a leak in the department. I don't doubt that

Lowicki's got some people there, but I'm positive he's unaware of the case we're building against him and Spencer. He's out in the open, showing himself all over town, acting as though he doesn't have a care in the world.

"We've learned some startling information about Lowicki and Spencer, Tuck. For one, they're part of a widespread organization that includes attorneys, bankers and people you'd never think of as criminals. It's big, Tuck, and has apparently been going on for some time right under our noses. The organization is in the drug market up to its eyeballs, and then laundering the money to clean up its act. We're gathering the evidence to make a major bust."

Tuck frowned thoughtfully. "There's an organization, all right, with plenty of dough to spread around. That cruiser out there on the lake is worth a good quarter of a mil." His mind was racing. If there wasn't a leak, then Lowicki and his pals had unearthed Nicole's identity through her car, which meant someone *had* followed them to Idaho.

"Joe, what about the Buckley murders? If Lowicki's such a big wheel in that organization, why would he risk his neck by killing two people in their own home?"

"The Buckleys were pushers, Tuck, not the ordinary citizens we initially believed. We think Lowicki and Spencer were at the Buckleys' apartment—not their real name, incidentally—to consummate a drug deal. Something went wrong and the shooting began. Forensics found evidence of a third person's blood. Either Lowicki or Spencer was hit, and we're pretty sure it wasn't Lowicki. It had to have been a superficial wound, as Spencer didn't show up at any of the hospitals. But he's got to have a wound someplace on his body, and if his blood matches what was found at the Buckleys' apartment, we've got him nailed."

"Sounds like you have enough evidence to pick them up right now."

"We do, but Spencer's underground somewhere, and besides, we want the whole organization. We're working as fast as possible, but we need a little more time. My concern now is for Nicole's safety. Can you move her to another location without discovery?"

"I'm sure as hell going to try," Tuck said grimly. "They tipped their hand today, Joe, and I've got a gut feeling they're going to come after us tonight. We've got to be gone before they get here. They won't move in until it's dark and they'll try to keep it quiet. We've got neighbors within yelling distance, so I think they'll try to sneak up on us in the middle of the night. As soon as it's dark, Nicole and I will leave, hopefully hours before they make their move."

"Tuck, maybe you should contact the Coeur d'Alene police for some backup help. What do you think?"

"That could end up bad, Joe. Any gunplay would be splashed all over the newspapers. We should keep this as low-key as possible."

"Yeah, you're right. Good luck, Tuck. Call when you can."

"I will."

Tuck put down the phone with a sober, brooding expression. At least they weren't sitting on their thumbs in Vegas. But was he as convinced as Joe that there hadn't been a leak of information? Some small mention of a witness who could place Lowicki and Spencer at the scene of the murders? Maybe those two felt that the police weren't aware of their "organization," and without Nicole's testimony, the D.A. wouldn't have a case against Lowicki. As for Spencer, maybe the third person's blood *wasn't* his. There could have been another party present at that fateful meeting, someone who left the building by another door. Or maybe lived in another apartment.

The possibilities were endless, which Tuck, after eleven years of law enforcement, knew wasn't abnormal. But however much evidence was being gathered about that organization's criminal activities, it was obvious that Nicole was still the prosecutor's strongest suit in the case against Lowicki and Spencer. Lowicki knew it, too, which was why he would stop at nothing to eliminate her.

Tuck's stomach muscles tensed. No one was going to "eliminate" Nicole, by God. He'd get her away from here and to a place of safety, and that was a vow.

He got up and strode down the hall to her bedroom door. Rapping on it, he called, "Nicole?"

"Come in."

Tuck opened the door. Nicole was sitting on the edge of her bed, looking emotionally ravaged. Her suitcases were on the floor near the closet, partially filled. There were clothes on a chair, as though her packing had suddenly lost steam and she'd just dropped them.

Her misery burrowed into his own system and became his to share. He knew how she felt—lost, helpless and frightened—and he didn't want her feeling that way. Automatically, so it seemed, he crossed the room and sat down next to her, putting an arm around her shoulders.

"Everything's going to be all right," he said, sounding confident for her sake. It didn't surprise him when Nicole laid her head on his shoulder and leaned into him. It was only natural for a deeply troubled person to seek comfort from another human being. He brought his free hand up to her head and stroked her hair. "We're going to get out of this, Nicole, I promise you. We'll be leaving right after dark."

He could feel the trembling of her body. She whispered tremulously, "Hold me, Tuck. Please hold me."

He turned slightly to bring her closer, and when he did her hands slid up his chest to the back of his neck. She pressed tightly against him, as though she'd like to crawl under his skin.

His heart started hammering. He'd intended only to offer comfort and their embrace was becoming sexual. Even knowing he should stop it here and now, he didn't. The woman in his arms felt like none other he'd ever held. Her scent was unique, as was the texture of her hair and skin.

She lifted her chin to look at him, and he saw the glaze of emotions gone wild in her beautiful blue eyes. In the back of his mind was a suspicion that she was in shock and not fully cognizant of what she was doing. But her upturned lips and beseeching expression weren't ignorable. Nor could he be so cruel as to turn his back on her when she needed him most. If that need had evolved into desire, so be it.

Besides, he wanted her. He couldn't remember when he'd wanted a woman more. Maybe the circumstances were wreaking havoc with his own emotions, as they were with Nicole's, but he suddenly knew he wasn't strong enough to get off this bed. Removing his gun from where he'd tucked it into his pants, he laid it on the nightstand.

Then he lowered his head until their lips met. The low moan in her throat threatened Tuck's sanity. He pushed her back on the bed and leaned over her, kissing her almost savagely. She responded in kind, with wild thrusts of her tongue and her body arching into his.

They began undoing buttons. Twisting and turning, kissing all the while, she pushed his shirt from his shoulders while he did the same with her blouse. He unzipped his fly and wriggled out of his jeans and underwear, kicking off his boots at the same time. Reaching down, he yanked off his socks. She had unbuttoned the waistband of her shorts, and he completed the job by pulling them down. Next went her bra and panties. Breathing hard, they turned on the bed so their heads were on the pillows.

Naked, their caresses were equal in intensity. Hungrily, her hands slid up and down his body. He left her lips to kiss and suck on her breasts. His mouth traveled downward, to the smooth, firm skin of her belly. They didn't speak. Their only sounds were groans and gasps of pleasure.

The pressure was building unbearably fast in Tuck, and he knew Nicole was feeling the same urgency when she moaned his name. "Tuck . . . Tuck . . ."

Without a word he reached down to the floor for the wallet in his jeans. In mere seconds he'd taken care of protection and was back in Nicole's arms.

Their kisses became frenzied. "Do it," she whispered raggedly. "Do it."

He slid into her feverish heat and had to grit his teeth to keep himself from an immediate climax. It had been too long since he'd been with a woman. Until now it hadn't mattered. But he was going to give Nicole the release she needed so desperately, even if the superhuman restraint necessary to do so killed him.

Restraint wasn't what Nicole wanted, however. She was writhing under him, demanding all he had to give. Her face was flushed and dewy. "Tuck . . ." It was a groan, a plea.

Her passion was destroying Tuck's good intentions. "Honey . . ." He tried to keep his desire in control by moving very slowly. But he was sweating and every nerve in his body was screaming for release.

She began moving with unmistakable impatience, squeezing him to herself, raising and lowering her hips at a faster tempo than he was attempting to maintain. Nicole was controlling this, he realized, not him, and she wasn't satisfied with slow and easy.

Well, neither was he. He let go then and rode her hard and fast. Her cries corresponded with the thrusts of his body. "Tuck . . . Tuck . . . *Tuck!*" He felt the spasms of her release begin a mere second before his own, and he continued to feel her pleasure after he had all but collapsed upon her, utterly drained.

Dazed, he could only think in bits and pieces. She was the most passionate woman he had ever made love with, the most exciting, the most beautiful.

But they shouldn't have done this. Not now, for God's sake, not when Lowicki's hired killers were just waiting for an opportunity to catch them off guard. Catch them with their pants down, he thought wryly, in this case, literally.

He lifted his head. Nicole's eyes met his. Reality was returning to her system, he realized. There was surprise in her eyes, along with bedazzlement and a strange sort of confusion.

"I . . . don't know what came over me," she whispered huskily. She had never spoken truer words. Her few sexual experiences hadn't even come close to what had just occurred between Tuck Hannigan and her. From a frightened, despairing woman, she had turned, in the blink of an eye, into a demanding, aggressive creature with only one thing on her mind. That she had succeeded so well was astounding. Almost as astonishing was Hannigan's participation. He, too, had done an incredible about-face.

But did he regret his loss of control now? She searched the depths of his eyes. What was she seeing, other than sheer masculinity and sexual satisfaction?

She laughed nervously, a brief sound without humor. "Say something."

Tuck wasn't eager to impart his thoughts. He'd stepped way over the line with Nicole, and in a dangerous situation, to boot. An army could have come crashing into the cabin a few minutes ago and he probably wouldn't have heard it. And he also knew what had "come over her," which she had questioned a minute ago. He had enough psychology in his background to understand that people narrowly escaping death and suffering the traumatic aftermath often sought affirmation that they were still alive and breathing. That was the reason she was under him now, the reason why she had turned to him with passion-crazed eyes and groping hands. If he explained that to her, though, she might not like it. She might not like *him*.

He wanted her to think well of him, which was a startling departure from his usual behavior with anyone, man or woman. Normally he didn't give a damn if someone liked him or not. With Nicole, it mattered.

Supporting his weight on one elbow, he tenderly touched her cheek. "I think something important just happened," he said quietly, hoping it was true. He'd been alone too long, and Nicole was making him feel like part of the human race again.

Her heart skipped a beat. It had been important to her, but him feeling the same was the last thing she'd expected to hear. She was ready to expand the topic, to tell him things about herself that she had discussed with no one else. For one, that she had never reached such heights with another man.

An inner, self-deprecating smile formed. Talking about other men wouldn't be wise right now, but she could probably get the message across without explicit details.

"Tuck..." Her expression was both dreamy and excited. But whatever words had been lined up to spill from her mouth were smothered by his kiss. It was a kiss of gentleness and warmth, and she forgot everything else and basked in it. His lips shaped hers, molded hers, and the gentleness gradually gave way to deeper emotions.

"I want to make love to you again," he whispered thickly.

"Yes," she murmured in a husky voice, willing to do anything he should suggest. Never could she have imagined the two of them together like this, but nothing in her life had ever been so phenomenal.

Then, stunning her, he abruptly turned back into a cop. "But not now."

Her eyes had become wide and startled, but he didn't notice as he'd left her and was getting off the bed, gathering his clothes.

"Finish your packing," he said. "It'll be dark in a few hours." He strode from the room.

Thunderstruck, Nicole stared after him. He was right, of course. They couldn't pretend they were a normal couple when they were about as abnormal as two strangers thrown together could be.

She attempted to revise that opinion almost immediately, wanting desperately to believe that it wasn't the two of them who were abnormal, but rather the situation.

Dear God, the crowning blow to this whole awful episode would be for her to fall in love with a man who really *was* abnormal.

What scared her was that she was already half in love with him. Great sex could do that to a woman, she thought while biting her lip to the point of pain. He had said he wanted to make love to her again, and she believed him because once was not enough for her, either.

But wasn't this a foolishly dangerous game for her be playing with a man of Hannigan's nature?

Nine

Tuck permitted himself the luxury of thinking about Nicole while he packed his things. She was strikingly pretty, intelligent, and incredibly exciting in bed. Those facts were strong and uppermost in his mind, but there were other things to remember, as well. The erotic shape of her hands and feet, for instance, the delicate swirl of her ears and the smooth, silky perfection of her skin. She was a very special lady, and it had been ages since he'd met one.

There were opposing factions in his brain over that knowledge: one was thrilled, the other wary. He'd been satisfied with bachelorhood since his divorce. Living alone was sometimes lonely, but for the most part he liked coming and going as he pleased. Those thoughts represented the wary side of the argument. The other side, the thrilled and expectant side, wasn't quite so cut-and-dried. Maybe his work wasn't enough anymore. Maybe the single life-style was beginning to wear thin.

When his suitcases were filled and latched, he determinedly turned his mind to the fix they were in and the risks they would be taking to get out of it.

His plan was to leave as soon as it was dark enough, and there were details he didn't dare overlook. Going outside, he sat in the driver's seat of the car with the door hanging open and turned on the radio loud enough for the sound to carry beyond the vehicle, flipping stations with one hand as though earnestly searching for one certain kind of music while unobtrusively unscrewing light bulbs with the other. When he and Nicole finally got in the car to leave, he didn't want any interior lights popping on and giving an onlooker a view he or she shouldn't have.

The possibility of state-of-the-art infrared equipment on that cruiser bothered him, but that was one of the risks they'd be taking. There was also the possibility of someone secreted on the mountain behind the cabin, another risk. What he had to bank on was their biggest threat coming from the front of the cabin, from the water, and then pray to God the scum watching them had only minimal equipment to rely on.

With every light inside the car out of commission, Tuck switched off the radio and slowly meandered back into the house, as though he didn't have a care in the world.

He couldn't load the car until nightfall, any more than he and Nicole could drive away until then. But there were still things to do in the cabin. Nicole had folded and put away the paper bags that the supermarket had used to transport the food they'd bought on their shopping trip. Locating the bags, Tuck unloaded the cupboards and filled the sacks.

He'd previously noticed an insulated ice chest in the Mathisons' laundry room, which he needed to borrow to hold the items from the refrigerator. There was plenty of ice as the fridge had an automatic ice maker. He would see that the Mathisons were reimbursed for the chest once he was back in Vegas and this godawful nightmare was behind them. For now, he couldn't worry about ethics and principles. He had no idea where he and Nicole would end up, but if they had food and water—he filled four gallon-size jugs—they could camp out, if necessary. Which, of course, meant filching some of the Mathisons' bedding.

He was creating a small mountain of luggage, food and bedding in the kitchen, he realized, standing back to frown at it all. It would take numerous trips from cabin to car to load it, and maybe that was too *much* risk.

Going down the hall, he rapped on Nicole's door. "Nicole? I need your help. Could you give me a hand?"

She opened the door, blushing slightly as she faced him for the first time since their wild lovemaking. She needn't have been concerned. Hannigan's expression wasn't even remotely personal.

"What do you want me to do?" she asked.

"Come to the kitchen." He took off.

Trailing behind him, she couldn't help admiring his physique. She'd seen him naked and touched him all over. His body was a work of art, completely masculine and utterly beautiful. The way the seat of his jeans was filled out was positively sinful. If he should suddenly turn around and suggest they return to the bedroom together, she'd go in a heartbeat, the mere thought of which made her pulse pump faster.

In the kitchen Tuck put his hands on his hips. "We need to sort through this stuff and bring it down to about a third."

Looking at the array before her, Nicole's jaw dropped. "You're taking the food? And the Mathisons' blankets?"

"Their ice chest is a must." Tuck went to the pile and moved the ice chest to one side. "So is the water." Over went the four gallon-size jugs. "But we can't take all of the food. Would you help me go through it and decide what's most important?"

She frowned. "I don't understand what you're doing."

"We might have to camp out for a few nights." His gaze became intense and bored into her. "I'm going to get you away from here, Nicole, but we might have to avoid the main roads for a while.''

"Have you studied the map? Do you know in which direction we'll be going?''

"East, into Montana. There's a lot of wilderness in western Montana. I'll find us a safe spot.''

The subject made Nicole uneasy. If she really dwelled on it, it made her *more* than uneasy. On the verge of screaming, actually. She trusted Hannigan, but did he know anything about "wilderness" and "camping out"? Her own knowledge wouldn't fill one sheet of paper—double-spaced.

Taking an unsteady breath, she looked at the items he had amassed. "Well ... I suppose the best thing to do is to take all the food out of the bags and start over,'' she said.

Tuck nodded. "Right, that's what we'll do. I've been thinking about our suitcases, too. Your four and my two add up to an awful lot of luggage.'' He moved to lean against the counter. "It's like this, Nicole. Once it's dark, we're going to have to load the car. Incidentally, do you have something in black you can wear?''

"I have black jeans and a long-sleeved sweatshirt.''

"Good. I'll be wearing black, too. Anyway, we can't go back and forth between the car and the cabin more than a few times.'' He eyed the bedding. "We have to have the blankets,'' he said, walking over to move them next to the ice chest and water.

Then he looked at her. "We're each going to have to make do with one suitcase. One *small* suitcase.''

"One! Tuck, other than formal wear and some of the things I wear to work, I brought practically every stitch I own. I can't leave all my clothes behind.''

"You can get them later, same as me. Sorry I told you to pack everything, but you're going to have to go through your suitcases and take only what you can't do without.''

She sighed heavily, demonstrating her reluctance on that score. But she would do as he asked, reluctant or not. "All right. Let's tackle the food first.''

Together they unloaded the paper sacks, made their choices, and then filled only two. Tuck stood back. "Okay, we have the ice chest, water, the bedding and two sacks of food. That'll keep us going for a few days. Go now and see to your luggage."

Nicole was depressed over this turn. At John Harper's advice she had packed for all variations of weather, other than winter. It was good that it *wasn't* winter right now, because her entire wardrobe—both here and in Vegas—did not include any cold-weather gear.

Sorting through her clothes in her bedroom, she crammed jeans, underwear, plain shirts, pajamas, a jacket and her cosmetic bag into her smallest suitcase.

In the kitchen Tuck returned the food they weren't taking with them to the cupboards. Glancing out the window he saw that at long last the sun was getting low on the horizon. He knew Nicole thought everything would be fine because they were leaving after dark, which was the way he wanted it. He hadn't talked about infrared scopes and such as there was little point to scaring her more than she already was over something she could do nothing about.

Physically his stomach muscles were as tense as a tightly coiled spring. Emotionally, though, he was prepared for their furtive departure. Now, more than ever, he was determined to keep Nicole safe.

Going to his bedroom, he emptied his two suitcases and repacked the smallest with the bare essentials. Then he changed into black jeans and T-shirt and slid his gun into the holster at the small of his back. Picking up his suitcase and a black vest he'd left out to put on later, he returned to the kitchen.

He was ready to go.

Dressed all in black, Nicole entered the kitchen carrying her small suitcase. Tuck took it from her hand and set it near his own. His gaze washed over her outfit. "You look good in black."

She checked his outfit, jeans, T-shirt and vest, all in black. "So do you."

He cleared his throat. "I made some sandwiches and coffee. You'd better eat," he told her. "Keep up your strength. It could be a long night."

The air seemed electrically charged. They were both on edge over the night ahead, but sharing the same modest space with them was a memory of hot kisses and steamy sex.

Nicole picked up a sandwich. "How much longer till dark?"

"Another hour or so." Tuck reached for his cup of coffee and took a swallow. He couldn't seem to stop looking at her. Now that everything was ready to go, he found himself thinking of that surprising interlude on her bed again.

She took a few bites of the sandwich and laid it on a napkin on the counter, sighing in the process. "I guess I'm too keyed up to eat," she murmured.

"Understandable," he said softly.

His tone made her skin tingle, because it gave away his thoughts. So did the expression in his eyes. Before today she had thought his eyes to be the coldest she'd ever seen.

They weren't cold now. She couldn't move, not with him looking at her like that. He set down his cup and took the few steps that separated them. Sliding his hands around her waist, he stared down at her.

"When this is over..." he began.

"Yes? When this is over?" she prompted, her voice sounding husky and sensual. She saw his tongue flick to dampen his lips. "You're very different than I first thought," she whispered, lifting a hand to touch his jaw with her fingertips.

"I can say the same about you."

She let her hand drift down from his jaw, tracing the curve of his throat, and lower, down his chest to the waistband of his jeans. "I never expected..."

"Neither did I," he said hoarsely. Then he laughed, shortly, sharply. "Making love with you was the *last* thing I expected out of this trip."

"Are you...sorry about it?"

"Do I wish it hadn't happened, you mean?"

"Yes, that's what I mean."

His eyes probed hers, as though looking for answers. "It might have been better if it hadn't."

"For you?"

"No, for you." Releasing his hold on her, he backed away. "For both of us, I suppose. The timing's bad. We— *I've* got to keep a clear head."

"Sex sort of muddies the water, doesn't it?"

His expression became slightly cynical. "Yeah, it does."

Nicole turned to pinch a piece of bread and meat from her sandwich. "Do...do you have a...girlfriend in Vegas?"

"No wife, no girlfriend. How about you?"

"No husband, no boyfriend," she said quietly, though her heart was beating a mile a minute. If he asked her to undress right here in the kitchen, she would do it. She'd almost started undressing him when her hand had been at the waistband of his jeans. She had it bad for Officer Tuck Hannigan, or was what she was feeling more accurately phrased by saying that she had it good? Was it good or bad to want a man so much that she was willing to undress for him if he should merely hint at feeling desire for her body?

He wasn't hinting, though certainly there'd been something sexual in his mind when he'd taken her by the waist.

The natural light in the kitchen was fading; the sun had dropped behind the mountains.

"It won't be long now," Tuck said, speaking low. "I'm going to do what I've been doing every night, turn on the porch lights. The front porch light, that is." He didn't dare turn on the back light as the car was parked within its range. "The idea is to make whoever's watching us think we're not alarmed and following the routines we've established since coming here."

"Makes sense," Nicole murmured rather absently. In truth, she wasn't at all engrossed in their escape, which God knew she should be. But with the dimming light, Hannigan's dark beauty, and the ache between her own legs, nothing else, not even the threat of those vultures out there, was strong enough to cool the fever searing the very marrow of her bones.

"Try to eat a little more," Tuck said in that same low tone before departing the kitchen to snap on the front porch light.

Wrapping her arms around herself, Nicole shivered as though chilled. *When this is over...* he'd said. Did that mean what she hoped it did? Was it possible he was becoming as obsessed with her as she was with him? Would he make love to her again right now if he wasn't waiting so intently for darkness to cloak the area? And then, when they returned to Vegas...

Well, it will happen one day, she thought defensively. Eventually this... this horror movie would be over and she and Hannigan would be home again.

Home. She groaned out loud.

Tuck walked in. "What's wrong?"

Apparently he'd heard the groan. "Talking about it won't make it right," she said while pouring herself a cup of coffee.

He studied her for a moment, then decided to drop the subject. She had more right to complain than anyone he'd ever known, but a discussion of what was wrong with their situation would only make it worse. At the very least, it would increase the tension they were both feeling.

"I turned the light on in your bedroom. A lamp in the living room, too," he said.

Nicole nodded in approval of his attempt to make everything appear normal in the cabin.

But the kitchen was dark and getting darker. "It won't be long now," Tuck said quietly.

Nicole sipped her coffee, then set down the cup. "I'm going to turn the light on in my bathroom for a few minutes." She managed a weak smile. "It's necessary."

Alone, Tuck forced himself into a chair. Waiting had never been easy for him. On any job he'd ever gone out on, the waiting had been the hardest part. Stakeouts had always been murderous to his nerves, and he'd weaseled out of stakeout duty whenever possible.

This was much too similar; waiting, sweating, wondering if he'd forgotten some tiny detail that would give his whole plan away in one fell swoop.

Nicole walked in. "The bathroom light's out again."

"Good. Lights going on and off will look good to..." He stopped.

"Don't avoid the obvious for my sake, Tuck. I know they're watching us."

"Yes, but why talk it to death?" He got up to peer into the dark backyard through the kitchen window. "Another few minutes," he murmured. "Then we'll get moving."

"Whenever you say," she said in a near whisper. Now that the time to leave was getting close, fear was again developing.

Tuck turned from the window. "I'm going out first... with the suitcases and the blankets. If everything feels all right, I'll come back in for the water jugs and the ice chest. Be prepared to follow me out with the food. Once outside, I don't want any talking. We'll get in the car, close the doors as quietly as possible and drive away without headlights."

"I understand." Just for something to do, she rinsed out their coffee cups and put them in the dishwasher. Then she wrapped the sandwiches Tuck had made and they hadn't eaten in paper napkins and tucked them into her shoulder bag. Her own observance of the back of the cabin was that it was black as pitch out there. She knew it was time to go before Tuck said so.

"I'm going out now with the first load," he told her. "Stand by the door." He started for the suitcases and blankets, then stopped to look at her. "If anything happens, run like hell. Head for the trees and keep on running." It wasn't great advice, but it was all he had to give her.

She tried to calm her racing pulse by breathing deeply. "I'm ready."

Tuck opened the door, then tucked his own suitcase under his left arm and picked up Nicole's with his left hand. With his right hand he stacked the blankets between his suitcase and chin, keeping the load on his left side so his right hand would be free to grab his gun. He went outside, quietly opened the back door of the car and put everything on the seat. Straightening, he looked around, taking his time, and saw nothing that shouldn't be there.

Returning to the cabin, he stacked the water jugs on top of the ice chest and picked up the unwieldy load. Nicole tossed the strap of her purse over her shoulder and lifted the food bags to her arms. The paper sacks crackled, making her skin crawl.

"Quietly now," Tuck whispered.

She nodded and silently followed him through the door and to the car. The water, food and ice chest were placed on the floor of the back seat, and Tuck motioned her to get into the car from the driver's door.

Then he froze. There were sounds, footsteps, distant and furtive but recognizable. Grabbing Nicole's arm, he stopped her from sliding into the car. She looked at him with startled eyes, but he was listening too intently to notice. Closing the doors of the car without even a click, he began dragging her away from the car and cabin.

She wanted to ask what he was doing, to question his actions, but she remained silent and permitted him to lead her into the trees and ultimately into the small storage shed that thus far had eluded her exploration.

When the door of the shed was shut, Tuck put his lips close to her ear and whispered. "There are two people out there, coming from the lake. Don't talk, don't move."

Nicole thought she might faint. She was either going to hyperventilate from fear or stop breathing altogether. Tuck whispered in her ear again. "There's a chance they don't know about this shed."

His thoughts went further. When those two killers discovered that the cabin was empty and the car was loaded for travel, they would start looking for them. The shed wasn't invisible, merely partially concealed by the heavy growth of timber and brush. If the two men searched at all, they would eventually stumble across it.

There was a high, small window on the east wall, and Tuck stood to one side of it with his gun drawn. "Get down," he whispered to Nicole. "Lie on the floor."

He didn't have to tell her twice. Nicole dropped at once, then lay there and worried about throwing up. The fear in her system was making her nauseous. She could just barely breathe and her heart was pounding so hard it hurt.

The shed smelled musty, of old wood and dampness. The floor wasn't clean; she could feel the dust and dirt under her hands. Instinct demanded flight, to get up and run. Passively awaiting death with her face on a dirty floor was ludicrous.

Cautiously lifting her head, she sent Hannigan a beseeching look. In the darkness he appeared as an even darker, statue-still silhouette. She could make out the gun in his hand, pointed upward. His attention was focused on the outside, not on her, her almost paralyzing fear or her physical discomfort.

"Tuck," she whispered plaintively. "Do you see anything?"

His head jerked around and he put a finger to his lips. It was a brief, staccatolike movement, taking up only a fraction of a second, and then he was squinting through the window again.

Two shadowy figures appeared at the top of the rise from the water. Tuck tensed. His eyes narrowed in speculation as they separated, one disappearing at the front of the cabin and the other creeping stealthily around to its hind side. They were going to rush the doors, he thought, one slamming through the front door, the other going through the back. It was good strategy for taking people by surprise.

Tuck lowered the barrel of his gun, aiming it at the person behind the cabin. He knew he could take him out with one shot, but he didn't pull the trigger. Sweat broke out on his forehead and under his arms. He could tell that the person was carrying something in his right hand, but he couldn't make out what it was.

It shocked him to see the person throw his weapon or parcel, whatever it was, through a window. The splintering of glass shattered the night silence, and then the person ran like hell, rounding the cabin only seconds before an explosion inside the cabin tore a portion of the roof off.

A second explosion came from the front of the cabin. "Sweet Jesus," Tuck muttered. The cabin was in flames. Debris from the explosions was falling everywhere, hitting the shed and the car. Panicked, Nicole jumped to her feet and grabbed Tuck's vest. Twisting around, he took her by the arm and steered her to the door. Opening it, he shoved her outside. "I've got to get the car. Start running for the road."

"No...no..." she moaned. "You'll get killed. The car..."

The car was too close to the flames. She knew it, he knew it. But without the car, they had no chance at all.

"Go!" He gave her a push, then turned his back on her and ran for the car.

Crying hysterically, Nicole stumbled up the drive toward the road. She could hear distant voices. The neighbors were already gathering. She was almost to the road when she heard the motor of the car start with a roar. He had made it. Tuck had saved the car.

Too weak to take another step, she clung to a small tree and watched the car speeding toward her. It screeched to a halt and the passenger door flew open. "Get in!" Tuck shouted.

Letting go of the tree, she fell into the car and yanked the door shut. Tuck gunned the engine and they took off fast. She turned to look through the rear window. Flames were shooting up higher than the trees. If they hadn't been outside when the bombs were thrown, they would both be dead.

Crumpling in the seat, she wept.

Ten

___

Tuck drove with the fiercest expression on his face that Nicole had ever seen on anyone. He'd taken the opposite direction from town, having learned from maps that the road followed the lake and joined up with a highway that had been the main east-west artery until the recent construction of a new freeway.

He would stay on the old highway, Tuck had previously decided. It would have a slower speed limit than the freeway, but it would also have access roads. One could get trapped on a freeway for many miles before finding an off ramp, and he wasn't going to be knowingly trapped by anything.

They still weren't in the clear. The lake road mostly threaded through the trees, but then, without warning, it would be right next to the water. Those were the miles that worried Tuck; the cruiser could be tracking them. If the people who'd thrown the explosives into the cabin had hung around at all, they'd seen him run for the car and drive it away from the burning building. Even if the cruiser wasn't tracking them, it would be a simple matter for the boss of those thugs to plant a vehicle at each end of the lake road, and the chase would begin again.

Tuck's most ardent hope was that the bomb tossers had been in a hurry to get away from the scene of their crime before the alarmed neighbors got too close, and hadn't noticed the car leaving. He would know that only when he reached the intersection with the old highway.

There was some light, oncoming traffic, but no one was behind him that he could detect. Still, he remained tense. Until they were off of this road, he couldn't relax his guard for a second.

Nicole's eyes had dried, but her spirit was so low she sat there like an automaton. The horrifying picture of the burning cabin was etched in her mind. If the explosions hadn't killed them, the flames would have. The Mathisons' cabin was destroyed, most of her clothes with it.

But she was alive and uninjured, thanks to Tuck. She turned her head to look at him and saw the same granite-like profile he had shown her during their long drive from Vegas. He was driving as though unaware of her presence, and she didn't want to interrupt his concentration by speaking. Sighing silently, she faced front again.

Tuck finally saw a sign announcing the intersection with the highway. His jaw clenched. This would tell the tale. If no black van, white sports car or some other vehicle was waiting for them, they would be home free. He held his breath while slowing down for the stop sign. As there were no cars coming from the left, he didn't completely stop but immediately made a right turn and picked up speed.

Elation zinged through him. No one had been waiting for them! They had made it. At long last he looked at Nicole.

"Are you all right?"

"You ran the stop sign."

He felt good enough about their escape to laugh a little. "Sure did." A glance in the rearview mirror surprised him. "Take a look out the back window."

She turned. "I can see the glow of the fire!"

"You can also bet there's chaos going on over there about now." A fire in that heavily treed area would draw a horde of fire fighters. If it spread from the cabin to the forest, a true disaster would be in the making. Besides, the neighbors would report the explosions, which would involve the police. Lowicki's people were still trying to make Nicole's death look like an accident, a freak explosion in this case, Tuck thought then, but using explosives had been a desperate measure and a dire mistake. The whole area would be crawling with investigators.

Nicole sighed. "I feel bad about the Mathisons' cabin."

"It wasn't your doing, Nicole. You didn't throw those bombs, whatever in hell kind they were."

"I know, but it was a nice cabin and it's not fair that the Mathisons should lose it."

"They'll be reimbursed." Tuck was keeping close watch on the rearview mirror. Traffic appeared only normal. No one was following them. "So will you, for your clothes," he added.

Nicole became thoughtful and spoke quietly. "Did we make it, Tuck? Did we really get away?"

"Right now I'm thinking yes. But we're going to play it very safe and stay alert."

"You're always alert," she murmured. Her head turned toward him. "I owe you so much. How can I thank you?"

"You owe me nothing. Don't think that way."

"You don't want my thanks? My gratitude? If I had stayed in Vegas, I wouldn't be alive, would I? And if you hadn't been at the cabin with me, I wouldn't be alive. Don't tell me I owe you nothing."

"I'll tell you what to be thankful for. Be thankful we still have the car," he said.

"Oh, I am. But that was your doing, too. Not only do we have the car, we have food and water. You're a thorough man, Officer Hannigan." A smile curved her lips, appearing without forethought. "I know exactly how to thank you."

He sent her a curious glance and caught on to her flirtatious mood. Considering how far down in the dumps she'd been only a few minutes ago, her change of attitude was astounding.

"You do, huh? What've you got in mind?" he asked teasingly.

She liked him like this. "I can't do it now, so you'll just have to wait and find out what it is later on." She suddenly noticed the dirt on her clothes. "Good grief, would you look at this," she exclaimed while beating the dust from her jeans and sweatshirt. "The floor of that shed was filthy."

"Not filthy, Nicole, just dusty."

"Well, it's all over me, whatever it was. I must look terrible."

"That's one thing you never have to worry about," he said. "You couldn't look terrible if you tried."

She cocked an eyebrow. "Was that a compliment?"

"Nope. That was the truth."

She wanted to slide across the seat and snuggle up against him. The thought was so strong in her mind, she could actually see herself doing it. She would slip her arm around his waist. He would lift *his* arm and let her lay her head on his shoulder.

Her heart skipped a beat. She was falling in love with Tuck Hannigan. He was what every man should be: strong, courageous, smart, and on the right side of the law. He was also a hot, tempestuous lover and incredibly handsome. No question about it, she was falling hard and fast.

But if she had no questions about her own feelings, there were plenty of them in her head about Tuck's. So he was courageous, strong, smart and incredibly handsome. Those qualities didn't guarantee that his lovemaking meant more than great sex to him. He could be a guy to take what was offered and even like her for it. But love? Love was a whole other ball game. Love meant commitment and lots of attached strings. One thing Tuck wasn't, was easy-going. He was hard and tough and cautious. There had to be a reason for him having no wife or girlfriend. Probably not the same reason why she had no husband or boyfriend, but he had a reason, make no mistake.

The painful truth was that she really didn't know him, except superficially. What she did know about him, she liked, but everyone had their quirks and own unique layers of personality. Scratch Hannigan's tough exterior and she might find a heart of gold.

But she also might find indifference and self-indulgence. She closed her eyes, shaken by the thought.

The car had stopped, waking Nicole with a start. Wherever they were parked, it was so black she could see nothing.

Tuck realized that she had awakened. Yawning, he reached into the back seat for a blanket. "I'm going to catch an hour's sleep."

"Where are we?"

"Somewhere in western Montana. I got off the highway. We're about half a mile down a dirt road in some real heavy timber." He was bunching the blanket, shaping a pillow to lay against the window for his head. "Go back to sleep. No one followed us. We beat 'em, Nicole."

"I've never been in such total darkness before," she murmured uneasily.

"Take a look." He flashed on the headlights. "See? Nothing to be afraid of."

They were surrounded by enormous trees seemingly connected to one another by thick underbrush. The headlights went off and Tuck settled his head against the blanket with a weary sigh.

"I must have slept a long time," Nicole said.

"Quite a while," Tuck replied drowsily. He opened his eyes and tried to see her. Her location was more sensation than sight; she was right about the total blackness, and he remembered that she had never claimed to be brave. "Come over here," he said quietly.

"You're sure? I don't want to keep you awake."

"I'm sure. Come on. Slide over."

"Thanks." Gratefully she slid across the seat and into his arms. She hadn't expected the embrace, but she melted into him as though she had. His body felt warm and wonderful in the dark, and she nestled as close as she could get.

"Careful," he said, sounding not quite as drowsy as he had a moment ago. "Or neither one of us will get any sleep."

"Sorry," she whispered, which was a lie as she wasn't sorry at all. Her very skin ached for the touch of his hands, and it might be selfish of her to hope he wouldn't fall asleep right away, but she couldn't help her thoughts.

She laid her cheek on his chest and listened to the hard, fast beating of his heart. When he squirmed and tried to get more comfortable, she knew he was becoming aroused. She heard him swallow, then clear his throat. He was trying to stay cool and it wasn't working. She had to smile.

"To hell with it," he muttered, finding her face with his hand to tip her chin up. He had no trouble at all locating her mouth with his, and his kiss was hard and hungry and maybe a little bit angry. Then he mumbled thickly, "This was not what I had in mind while looking for a place to stop for an hour or so."

"I know," she whispered. But at the same time she was opening his jeans.

"Nicole," he groaned when she began stroking him.

In her mind's eye she could see what she was caressing, and the combination of touch and imagery was so exciting she couldn't sit still.

Neither could Tuck. They started groping for each other's buttons, pulling and tugging clothes around until they were both naked enough. They moved over on the seat, away from the steering wheel, and she straddled his lap, kissing his mouth with feverish desire while gently lowering herself onto his erect and rock-hard manhood. His big hands gripped her buttocks, dictating her movements, while his own hips rose and fell to maintain their perfect rhythm.

"Damn, we're good together," Tuck growled deep in his throat. "Do you know *how* good?"

"I know how good it is for me," she whispered, her lips brushing his while she spoke. In the dark she could be bold. "It's never been so good with anyone else, not ever."

That was a statement to make any dyed-in-the-wool bachelor do a little sweating, and Tuck knew he'd take it out and give it some thought when he had the time. Right now, thinking at all was damned near impossible. Everything was sin and sensation, hot pleasure in a coal black night. He was lost in sensation, drowning in it.

Breathing raggedly, he felt the beginning of the end for him. "Stay with me, baby," he said hoarsely.

They were rocking the car with their frenetic energy, moaning and panting and climbing to the heights together. "I'm with you," she gasped. She *was* with him, and she suspected it would always be like this for them, given the chance, that is. How much longer would they have to stay away from Vegas? A day? A week? A month?

She prayed for at least another week together, though the prayer was brief and almost immediately forgotten. In its place were the words *I love you.* They were so crisp and delineated in her mind that for a moment she thought she had said them out loud.

The end was blinding for her, draining her of strength and mobility. She fell forward at the same moment Tuck roared her name. *"Nicole!"* His hands dropped to the seat, limp as a dishrag. He put his head back and nearly fell asleep on the spot.

Nicole stirred first, sitting up to press a gentle kiss to his lips. "Nicole," he said in a barely audible voice. "I'm too tired to move."

"Then I will." She untangled their bodies and slid to the seat. Tuck wasn't wriggling even a finger, and she straightened his clothes the best she could, then got out of the car to tend to herself. They hadn't used protection, and it was up to her to do what little she could about that oversight, even if it meant braving the black forest all by herself.

Tuck opened his eyes to daylight and was immediately irritated with himself, as he'd only intended to sleep for an hour. Feeling cramped, he sat up straighter to relieve his aching body, and to look around. The road contained spots of sunshine, but the dense forest on each side of the car was dim and shadowy, except for the tops of the tall trees, which seemed to be lifting to the sun. It was beautiful country, silent and seemingly separate from the rest of the world.

Nature called. Realizing that he was covered with a blanket, he pushed it aside so he could get out of the car. He frowned then, because he was only half dressed.

Memory came rushing in. Without his disheveled clothing as evidence, he would have thought last night's sexual encounter to be a dream. He turned his head to look at Nicole, who had lowered the back of her seat sometime in the night and was presently wrapped in a blanket. Her eyes were open and watching him.

"Good morning," she said softly. "Do you know that you're even handsome in the morning, with whisker stubble on your face and sleepy eyes?"

The affection in her expression gave Tuck pause. Things were happening too fast between them. He liked her. Hell, maybe he even loved her. But that was now. They were locked into an unusual situation, and he couldn't start spouting guarantees about how he would feel about her or anything else when this was over. Surely she must know that for herself.

"I'm going outside for a few minutes," he stated tonelessly, completely ignoring her blarney about him looking handsome with whisker stubble and sleepy eyes. Opening the door, he stepped out into the cool morning air.

Nicole pushed the lever that brought her seat back forward and watched him walk into the trees. Thoughtfully she folded the blankets they had used and got on her knees to lean over the seat to lay them in the back. Opening her suitcase, she took out her cosmetic case, then dug into it for her toothbrush and toothpaste. Realizing that her position was too awkward to reach the water jugs, she got out and opened the back door of the car.

When Tuck returned, she was brushing her teeth, using the water she had poured into a paper cup. "I'd give my right arm for a bath," she said, merely to make conversation.

"Me, too," he said, merely to give her an answer.

It was Nicole's turn to disappear into the trees. Tuck brushed his teeth and pondered their next move. He was still feeling out of sorts over sleeping so long and so soundly. Anyone could have come up on them and he wouldn't have known about it until it was too late.

Where were they, exactly? Getting out the atlas, he opened it on the hood of the car and studied the map of Montana. Following last night's route with his forefinger, he decided they were on a road that wasn't even on the map. It probably wasn't a road at all, not one for public usage, at any rate.

Glancing at the tall timber, he nodded to himself. They were on a logging road, one that hadn't been in use for a good long time by the look of it. Certainly there wasn't any logging going on in this particular area at the present.

But he pretty much knew where they were on the map now, and the question was where to go from here. This part of Montana seemed to have quite a few small towns. It didn't really matter where they ended up, and in fact, staying on the move for another day or two might be best. But he couldn't avoid towns altogether, nor could they sleep in the car again. He was stiff and sore from just one night, and Nicole had to be, too. Although he'd mentioned camping out, they really weren't equipped for sleeping under the stars.

Nicole came strolling back. "This place is really beautiful," she remarked. "How did you find it?"

"Followed my nose, I guess." Tuck found it difficult to look directly at her. There was too much between them for pretense, and yet he didn't know what it meant or even if it meant anything at all. The one thing he didn't want was her thinking they were falling in love when he was so uncertain.

"Well, your nose has good instincts," she said with a teasing smile. She wished he would smile back at her, but he didn't. In fact, his expression was remote and his mood rather grumpy.

After yesterday's harassing events, the serenity of this place felt like heaven to Nicole. She was determined to be cheerful in spite of Tuck's unsmiling countenance.

"How about some breakfast?" she said, leaning into the back seat of the car for the sacks of food. Tuck continued to study the map without replying, so she took out a couple of oranges, a loaf of bread and then went into the ice chest for a package of sliced smoked turkey.

She peeled both oranges, made sandwiches, and brought a paper plate of food and a cup of water to Tuck. "Thanks," he mumbled.

"You're welcome." Nicole found a tiny patch of grass a few feet from the car, spread out one of the blankets and sat down with her breakfast. Her gaze remained on Tuck while she ate. He was eating absently, intent on the map and seemingly deep in thought.

"So, what's next on the agenda?" she finally asked, feeling she had every right to know what he was concentrating so hard on. She suspected he was trying to ignore or forget what had happened between them last night, which hurt. She might be falling in love, but he certainly wasn't. She really must be more realistic about their relationship, she thought with a painful tugging of her heart.

He sent her a glance. "I'm going to have to find a phone and call Joe Crawford. The Mathisons must have been told about their cabin by now. If they called Joe and told him about it—which only makes sense—he's probably frantic."

Thoughtfully, Nicole nodded. "Yes, he must be terribly concerned. But once the fire was out, wouldn't the police, or whoever, be able to tell that there wasn't anyone in the cabin when it exploded?"

"No bodies? Yeah, they'd know that. But no charred bodies isn't a guarantee that we got away."

"No, I suppose not," Nicole murmured. "Lowicki's people know we did, though. I mean, if it was spread around that the fire caused no fatalities, they have to know we escaped their desperate attempt to…to eliminate us." She swallowed hard, suddenly nervous again. This place felt safe, but was it? Was any place?

Tuck sensed her returning concern. "Don't worry, okay? They probably know we got away by now, but they couldn't possibly know where we went. Besides, they've got their own butts to worry about now. I'm betting they got the hell out of Coeur d'Alene immediately after the explosions."

"You really think so?"

Tuck's scowl surprised her. "You know what really galls me? *Letting* them get away with it."

"You didn't *let* them do anything!"

"The hell I didn't. I had one of them…" He stopped. He could have shot the creep sneaking around the back of the cabin and hadn't done it. Would he have pulled the trigger if last night's events had happened before he'd killed those two men in that convenience store holdup? He'd thought a lot about that last night while he was driving and Nicole slept.

There was a sudden uncomfortable knot in his stomach. "Let's get going," he said brusquely.

Nicole frowned at him. "Are you angry with me about something?"

"No."

She got up from the blanket. "Well, you sound like it." Carrying her paper plate and cup, she walked over to take Tuck's.

He drew a long breath. She was too perceptive for lies. "I am angry, but not with you."

She was close enough to him to look into his eyes. "Since we're the only ones out here, if you're not angry with me, then you must be angry with yourself. For God's sake, why? You saved both of our lives last night. What more do you think you should have done?" She remembered what he'd just said about letting them get away with it. "You're not really thinking that you should have confronted those two killers, are you?"

His mouth twisted cynically. "I've never run from danger before."

"You retreated, Tuck, you didn't run. And don't forget that you had me on your hands. You wouldn't have retreated if I hadn't been hanging on your shirttail."

He had to admit the truth of her argument. Until he got the "all clear" from Joe and they could return to Vegas, his first consideration was Nicole, in any setting or situation. That was what had been on his mind last night, getting her out of there and away from danger. He'd done the right thing.

But it still rubbed him wrong, and he would welcome a face-to-face with any of Lowicki's people anytime, anywhere. Once Nicole was out of the picture, that is.

They got in the car. Tuck managed to turn it around on the narrow road and they headed back for the highway. Everything looked different in the daylight, Tuck realized, seeing a fence line he'd missed last night. They approached the back of a sizable sign, which he'd also missed seeing in the dark.

Nicole swiveled in her seat to see what was on the sign. "Stop for a minute, Tuck," she exclaimed.

He put on the brakes. "What is it?"

She read out loud. "'House, barn and five acres for rent. Seven miles ahead. Three bedrooms, one bath. All utilities. Call 555-7787.'" She looked at Tuck. "Maybe we should check that out. It might be a good place to stay until Captain Crawford says it's okay to go home. What do you think?"

"Write down the number. Do you have something to write on?"

"In my purse." Nicole dug into her purse, then wrote down the telephone number on a scrap of paper. The car began moving again. "No one would ever find us out there," she said.

No one would if they didn't make themselves obvious in the area, Tuck thought grimly. Was the house empty? He suddenly slammed on the brakes and began turning the car around again.

Nicole's eyes widened. "What're you doing?"

"We're going to take a look at that house."

"Oh. Well, I guess that makes sense. Maybe it's an awful place."

"Yeah, maybe." But that wasn't what was in Tuck's mind. If the house was empty, they might just "borrow" it for a few days without contacting the owner. Then no one would know where they were for certain. He would, of course, make sure that the owner was well paid for the use of his house, once this was over.

They passed the spot in the trees where they had made love and slept, and kept going with neither of them remarking on it. The forest went on and on, and they were able to pick out areas that had once been logged.

"There haven't been any loggers in here for years," Tuck said, noticing how the brush had grown up around old, weathered tree stumps. The farther they drove, the worse the road became, deeply rutted in places and all but washed away in others.

"The paint on that sign was really faded, Tuck," Nicole said. "Maybe it was put up years ago and the owner neglected to take it down. The house couldn't possibly have been vacant all that time, could it?"

"Anything's possible." This setup was looking better and better to him. If someone was living in that house, the road would show signs of usage, and he would bet anything that this car was the first vehicle over it in a very long time.

The trees gave way without warning. One second they were surrounded by dense forest and the next they were in a sunshine-bright clearing. Weeds and wild grass were two to three feet high, all the way to the ramshackle house and barn. Rusted logging equipment resided next to the barn. The place was glaringly vacant.

"Well, well," Tuck murmured under his breath. Nicole sent him a curious glance, but he was cautiously avoiding potholes on the ancient road and missed seeing it.

"It doesn't look like much," Nicole said. The house was sided with rough lumber, which had turned an unsightly gray-brown from time and weather. It had a sagging front porch and several broken windows. "It really *is* awful," she added, recalling that she had speculated on that very idea.

Tuck parked next to the house and turned off the motor. "I'm going to take a look at it. Coming?" He got out of the car.

She hesitated, then followed him out.

"There's one thing in its favor," Tuck stated emphatically. "No neighbors." He looked at Nicole. "Come on. Let's explore."

Eleven

The front door wasn't locked. Tuck pushed it open. "Hey, it's got furniture," he exclaimed.

Nicole looked at the "furniture" and gulped. First of all, everything was covered in dust and cobwebs, the old, worn, olive green shag carpet, the ugly brown sofa and green chair, the scarred end tables and dime-store lamps. The room had one redeeming feature, a large, lava-rock fireplace. There was also, she noted, a monstrous heating stove in one corner of the room.

"It's terrible, Tuck," she said with a grimace and a wrinkling of her nose. It even smelled dirty.

"Pretty bad, all right," he agreed. "Let's see the rest of it."

They walked into the kitchen. There was a wood-burning cook stove, an ancient refrigerator, a sink and small counter, and a round table with four chairs.

"Other than in museums, I've never even seen a stove like this," Nicole said, moving closer to the thing to look at it.

Tuck had to laugh at her shocked tone of voice. He turned a water faucet and nothing happened. "I wonder how they get water into the house," he mumbled to himself. The faucets proved that the place had some sort of plumbing system, but it sure wasn't what he was used to. He'd have to investigate that problem. "I want to see the bedrooms and bath," he told Nicole.

They traipsed through the bedrooms, each containing a bed, a dresser and a minuscule closet, and then the small bathroom, which was equipped with a stained metal shower stall, sink and toilet.

Nicole didn't like the glint in Hannigan's eyes. "Tell me you're not really considering renting this place," she said.

"It could be cleaned up," he said.

"You *are* considering it! Tuck, it's horrible."

"But it's off the beaten path."

That was true, but how could she bear staying in such a terrible place? "What about utilities? The sign said that it had all of the utilities, but it doesn't." She frantically worked a wall switch. "See? No lights."

"The only utility we'd have to have is plumbing. I suspect there's a well and some kind of equipment to draw the water into the house."

"And you think it would work? Tuck, no one's lived here for years. Any equipment would be long out of commission."

"Maybe, maybe not."

Nicole felt like crying. "Well, I don't like it. It's awful and dirty and . . . and I can't cook on a wood stove."

"I can." He saw her forlorn expression, but couldn't give in to the sympathy he felt. Lowicki's people could search for them for ten years and never find them here. Even the owner of the house hadn't been here in years. No one had. It was a perfect place to hide out for a while.

"Let's go," he said.

Nicole nearly collapsed with relief. "Then you're not going to rent it?"

"Nope." Tuck was on his way out, with Nicole on his heels. "We're going to find a phone, then a store to buy food, some cleaning supplies and a few tools."

Nicole stopped dead in her tracks. "Why?"

Tuck turned to face her. "Because we're going to move in."

"Without telling the owner?"

"Without telling anyone." He started walking again. Reaching the car, he got in and started it.

Nicole got in with an angry expression. "Obviously I have nothing to say about it."

"Obviously."

"You know, you can be a real pain in the neck when you want to be."

He turned the car around and sent her a look. "What happened to 'Thanks for saving my life, Tuck'?"

"You said you didn't want thanks," she retorted.

"And you said you were going to cooperate," he reminded her.

Her eyes snapped. "When I said that we were living in a very pleasant cabin, not in a pigsty."

"It won't be a pigsty after it's cleaned."

"And who's going to do the cleaning?"

"Who's the one complaining about the dirt?"

"You expect *me* to clean that . . . that hovel?"

"It'll give you something to do while I'm figuring out the plumbing system."

Mentally she called him some vile names. What Tuck saw from her was a sullen, petulant expression and a pair of angrily folded arms.

He frowned. "Nicole, you have to trust my judgment on this."

She knew it was true, and she also knew his judgment was sound. But that awful house gave her the heebie-jeebies. She wasn't afraid of some hard work to clean it up, but it was in the middle of nowhere. And while Tuck might figure out the water system and even get it operational, they wouldn't have electricity. Maybe it was snooty of her to feel so appalled at the idea of staying there, but there was a limit to what she should have to endure.

And yet... Frowning while Tuck drove, Nicole thought about how alone they would be out there. Hadn't she been hoping for more time together? Certainly very little would stand in the way of their getting to know each other. Once the place was clean and livable, all they would have to focus on would be each other.

She sat straighter and unfolded her arms. "Maybe it wouldn't be so bad," she said slowly.

Tuck's head jerked around to send her a look. "What brought that on?"

"Well, as you said, I have to trust your judgment, and I really do, Tuck. If you think staying out there is best, then it probably is."

"Hmm," he said, sounding thoroughly puzzled. But thinking rationally, he hadn't known Nicole long enough to understand her. She had to feel the same about him, of course. Odd that they had made love twice and didn't really know each other. And he was positive Nicole wasn't a woman who passed out her favors indiscriminately. He'd come in contact with that type of woman enough to recognize the species, and Nicole simply didn't fit the mold.

A nervous tweak gave him a start. What if she *had* fallen for him, as in, fallen in love? If it had happened, it was only because of their circumstances, he told himself uneasily. Because they'd been thrown together in a situation where she had to depend on him. Dependency could cause admiration and even affection.

He smirked wryly. That might explain Nicole's attitude toward him, but what explained his treatment of her? He sure hadn't made love to her because of dependency. He'd made love to her because she was...special. The word hung in his mind like a helium-filled balloon. *Special.*

"Oh, there's a gas station," Nicole exclaimed. "And it has a pay phone." Tuck drove on by. "I thought you were going to call Captain Crawford?"

"I am, but not from that phone. If we're going to stay in that old house, we're not going to make ourselves known to anyone in the vicinity."

"Oh." Nicole fell silent for a moment. "It's at least fifteen miles back to that house, Tuck, hardly in the vicinity."

"That service station is the closest business to that place. We won't ever be stopping there."

She sighed. They thought so differently. She never forgot that he was a cop, but there were times, like now, that their differences seemed to be spelled out in capital letters.

Tuck avoided the interstate and took back roads to a pleasant little community about thirty miles from the service station they had driven by. He slowly cruised the streets until he found the busiest corner in town. There was a fast-food restaurant, a gas station and a grocery store, all in one small area. There were lots of people and cars...and two pay phones in front of the grocery store. He pulled into a parking space.

"Wait here," he said as he got out.

Nicole watched him stroll across the parking lot to one of the phones. With so much activity in the immediate vicinity, no one paid him any mind. It was what he had wanted, she realized. To blend with the environment, to appear as an ordinary citizen making an ordinary phone call. He thinks of everything, she thought with a slight frown. Were his instincts unique, or was every experienced cop as clearheaded and alert as Tuck Hannigan?

Using his own personal credit card to pay for the call, Tuck dialed Joe's private number. He'd been lucky so far about reaching Joe, Tuck thought through several rings. Joe wasn't always in his office, and no one else had the authority to answer this particular number.

He heaved a sigh of relief when the phone was picked up on the fifth ring. "Crawford."

"It's Tuck, Joe."

"Tuck! Man, I've been walking the floor since last night. Where in hell have you been? Why didn't you call in sooner? I didn't know if you were alive or dead. Is Nicole all right?"

"Nicole's fine. Obviously you were notified about the explosion."

"Obviously," Joe said dryly. His tone changed. "Thank God the two of you weren't at the cabin."

"We were there, only we weren't inside. It's a long story, Joe. What's going on in Vegas?"

"So much that I don't know where to begin. First of all, you two can come home now."

"You're kidding! You mean it's over?"

"Damned near. The fat lady'll do her singing in court, Tuck. We made a major bust around 1:00 a.m. last night. Picked up Lowicki and..." Joe recited a list of names, some of which caused Tuck to whistle in amazement. Joe went on. "Gil Spencer's dead. He *was* shot the night of the Buckley murders, and was too damned scared to go to a hospital. Anyway, he's history. I'll go into the gory details of that episode when you get back. One thing more. The Coeur d'Alene police nailed the jokers in that cruiser, including the two people who fired the cabin. One of them was—take a guess—Jillian Marsden. Seems the cops in Coeur d'Alene were keeping an eye on the cruiser for their own reasons. Take another guess—drugs. Anyway, they got the bastards and so did we. Come on in, Tuck. Bring Ms. Currie home safe and sound. The prosecutor's chomping at the bit to talk to her."

"We'll leave as soon as we get organized."

"Where are you now?"

"In western Montana. I'm not going to drive straight through this time, Joe. Our trip north was too hard on Nicole. So we should be pulling into Vegas sometime tomorrow."

"Okay. Report in when you get here."

"Do I take Nicole to her home, or what?"

"Well . . . she'll probably be too tired to face a barrage of questions immediately after a long trip. Yeah, take her to her house. It's safe now."

"You're sure about that."

"Tell you what. She might not feel safe, so when you get here and report in, I'll put a car and a couple of men on her house."

"Good idea. She's apt to be nervous at first. Well . . . see you tomorrow, Joe."

"Right. Incidentally, tell her that I talked to her employers. Did it myself so there wouldn't be any misunderstanding. Her job is waiting for her. And, Tuck, thanks for doing a hell of a piece of work. You'll get a commendation out of this."

"Uh, great. Fine. 'Bye, Joe." Tuck hung up.

Nicole saw him hang up the phone, then wondered why he didn't immediately head for the car. He seemed to be thinking, just standing there thinking. Her heart started pounding. Oh, God, what had happened now?

Finally he began walking toward the car. Nicole's anxiety level rose with each step he took. His expression was dark and brooding again, making her imagination run wild. What had Captain Crawford told him to cause that dour look on Tuck's face?

He opened the door, sat behind the wheel and pulled the door shut, all without looking at her. Nicole slid across the seat and put her hand on his arm.

"What is it, Tuck? What's happened now?"

His head turned slowly toward her. She was so pretty and he felt her deep inside of himself, in a place no one else had ever occupied. *Special*.

"It's over," he said quietly. "We're going home."

"*What?*"

"They've arrested everyone involved, including our stalkers in Coeur d'Alene. The prosecutor wants you back in Vegas as soon as possible."

The breath left Nicole's body in one big whoosh. She fell back against the seat.

"I thought you'd be thrilled," Tuck said.

"I—I am."

She didn't look thrilled. She looked disappointed and rather miserable, pretty much the way he felt.

"Tell you what," he said. "We both need a bath and a little rest before we leave. How about renting a motel room for a few hours? Then we'll get a good meal at a restaurant and start out fresh." He paused, remembering that there was no longer a reason to pretend they were a married couple. "We'll get two rooms," he said, watching her closely while he spoke.

Her eyes widened in surprise, then the reality of their altered situation sank in. It was over; the fear, the excitement, the living on the edge. For some bizarre reason she felt as though someone or something had let the air out of her.

"All right," she said in a tight little voice. "I really would like to shower and get into some clean clothes."

"Right."

Tuck drove around the small town until he located a motel that struck his fancy. It was constructed of red brick with white wood trim and looked well cared for. He turned into it and stopped the car next to the office. Without further conversation on the matter, he got out and went into the office.

Nicole blinked at the sting of tears in her eyes. What in God's name was wrong with her? she had to ask herself. She should be turning handsprings instead of feeling as though the bottom had dropped out of her world.

But now they wouldn't be cleaning that awful house and have the opportunity to "focus" on each other. They would drive back to Vegas and, once there, go their separate ways. The feelings she had for Tuck weren't going to conveniently vanish at the Las Vegas city limits. The truth was, she would never get over him, and it wasn't fair.

"Damn, damn, damn," she mumbled. She had fought against leaving Vegas and now she didn't want to return. Her change of heart was due to Tuck, and it wasn't fair. She hadn't asked for heartache, certainly hadn't gone looking for it, but she was stuck with it, and it wasn't fair.

Tuck came out with two keys, one of which he handed to her when he got into the car. In oppressive silence, he drove to the far end of the motel and pulled into a parking slot in front of Room 115.

Nicole glanced at her key. Number 116. Their rooms were side by side.

There didn't seem to be anything to say. They got out, retrieved their suitcases from the back seat and Tuck locked the car.

"Well..." Nicole said. "See you later."

Tuck looked at the ground for a moment, then lifted his eyes to hers. "Yeah, see you later. Knock on the door if you need anything."

"You, too."

Inside room 116, Nicole set down her suitcase and threw herself onto the bed, lying on her back to stare at the ceiling. It didn't seem possible that everything was back to normal so suddenlike. It hadn't been months, as Detective Harper had warned her could happen, or even weeks. They had moved fast in Vegas, which she'd been assured would be the case. Yet she really hadn't expected such haste as this. She would have some explaining to do to her employers, but more than likely even her job wasn't in jeopardy.

The ceiling was smooth white paint, and it appeared as a large, blank artist's canvas or a movie screen. Nicole's imagination provided the images, herself in her home, at her desk in the Monte Carlo, seeing her friends, doing all of the things she had enjoyed before this major interruption of her life.

Before meeting Tuck Hannigan, she thought grimly. Her former routines seemed dull as dishwater now. How could she just go on as though their time together had never happened? As though they hadn't made the most incredible love known to mankind?

Her eyes narrowed then. Tuck didn't seem to be in any particular hurry to get back to Vegas, either, did he? His suggestion to rent rooms so they could clean up and rest for a few hours before leaving was really very surprising, and not at all what she'd come to expect from him and his dedication to duty.

"Hmm," she murmured. Was it possible his thoughts were paralleling hers this very minute?

Her spirit lifted suddenly and she got off the bed and started shedding her dirty clothes. That was when she took notice of the room. Decorated in a deep rose color with white accents, it was a very pleasant room.

But its most interesting feature, by far, was the door in the contiguous wall of the two motel units, rooms 115 and 116.

Smiling, she headed for the bathroom and shower.

The light rapping on Tuck's side of the connecting door brought a smile to Nicole's lips. She was dressed, seated at the small table under the room's one window, and had just finished applying a coat of clear polish to her fingernails. It felt good not to have to shy away from windows anymore, and Nicole had pulled the drapes wide open. The room was bright with natural daylight.

Rising, she opened her side of the door cautiously, so as not to smudge the wet polish on her nails.

"Hi," she said. Tuck looked crisp from a shower and shave. He was wearing fresh jeans and a white shirt. A fluttering in her chest was no surprise.

"Hi. There's something I forgot to tell you," he said. His gaze washed over Nicole's snow-white jeans and royal blue blouse. Her hair was perfectly arranged and she was wearing makeup. The scent she was giving off was delicious, a delicate perfume that he could almost see her touching to her throat and other erotic points of her body.

"Come on in." She waved her hands. "Wet polish. It'll be dry in a few minutes." There were two chairs at the round table. Nicole resumed her seat and Tuck sank onto the other. She blew on her nails. "What was it you forget to tell me?"

Tuck blinked. He'd been so lost in Nicole's appearance and scent that everything else had fled his mind.

"Um . . . oh, yes. Joe Crawford said to tell you that he talked to your employers and your job is waiting for you."

Nicole blew on her nails again. "That's good news."

"You don't sound like it is."

She shrugged. "Sorry." Her eyes met his. "Apparently you anticipated a different response. Something girlish and giddy, perhaps? I don't feel girlish and giddy, Tuck."

"No?" He was watching her closely. "What *are* you feeling?"

She laughed briefly. "That's a loaded question. Are you sure you want an answer?"

After a long look at her, he got up to move around her room. Her suitcase was open, and he saw blue jeans, various colored tops and soft, silky underwear. His mouth went dry.

Swallowing to moisten his throat, he turned. "About your clothes. You should make a list of what was destroyed by the fire so the reimbursement will be as accurate as possible."

"It's going to be a large sum of money," she said evenly. "I don't buy inexpensive clothing."

"You must make good money."

"I do."

"Probably twice, three times what I make."

"Since I have no idea what police officers are paid, I really couldn't say."

It was a stupid conversation. Tuck didn't care what her income was and had no desire to discuss his own salary. He should return to his room, lie down and get some rest.

Still, he lingered. "Are you hungry? We could eat now and rest later."

"Or rest now and eat later?" Her direct and steady look contained a challenge that Tuck didn't miss. It sent a frisson of excitement up his spine.

"I'll leave it up to you. What do you want to do?" he asked softly.

"Another loaded question." Her voice was low and husky.

Her references to "loaded questions" raised Tuck's blood pressure. Obviously she was thinking of intimacy and rather boldly letting him know about it. He darted a quick glance at her bed, then jerked his eyes back to her. They were suddenly on the same wavelength.

Slowly, Nicole got to her feet. "What's happening with us, Tuck?" she asked in a near whisper as she took the few steps separating them. Standing in front him, she tilted her head to look into his eyes. When he merely looked back without answering, she said, "Do you know?"

He drew in a long, unsteady breath. She was close enough to touch, and touching was definitely on his mind. Talking about it wasn't, though. He had no answers to give her. None, for that matter, to give himself.

"Physical attraction, I guess," he mumbled thickly.

"An understatement," she murmured. "Do you know that thoughts of making love with you rarely leave my mind?" She stepped closer and laid her hands on his chest. Rising on tiptoes, she put her lips very close to his. "When we get back to Vegas, are you going to forget me, Tuck?"

He swept her into his arms almost angrily. Only a breath separated their faces. "I didn't come in here for this," he stated darkly.

Her eyes contained a woman's knowledge and a trace of laughter. "Yes, you did. This is exactly why..."

His mouth on hers stopped everything. She moved against him, lifting her hands to thread through his hair. His kiss conveyed urgency and desire, and she kissed him back in the same impassioned way.

Breathing hard, they tipped their heads back to look at each other. "Are you fighting with yourself over this?" she whispered hoarsely.

"It shouldn't be happening."

"Why shouldn't it?" Her hands slipped down to the front of his shirt, where she began undoing buttons. "Because you intend to forget me when we're home again?"

"I wish you wouldn't say things like that."

She had his shirt open, and she pressed her lips to the hot skin of his chest. He groaned. She was right. This was exactly why he'd knocked on that connecting door. He'd tried to rest after cleaning up and had even been lying down. But instead of sleeping, which he'd wholeheartedly wanted to do, he'd lain there thinking of Nicole, remembering last night and how wild their lovemaking had been.

Then he'd remembered what Joe had said about talking to Nicole's employers—a damned good excuse for knocking on that door.

"The first time we made love you said something important was happening between us," she whispered. "Now you're saying it shouldn't be happening. What should I believe, Tuck?"

He took her by the shoulders. His eyes burned into hers. "Believe that I want you. It's not something I can control. But believe, also, that it's not best for us."

She said nothing for a long time, and they just stood there and studied the emotion in each other's eyes. Then, quietly, huskily, she spoke. "Shall I pull the drape?"

Twelve

Tuck checked his watch in the dim light of the room. Nicole was snuggled next to him. Dozing, he thought. They had been in her bed for more than an hour, and his entire system was saturated with the aftermath of breathtaking sex.

They were going to have to leave soon, get something to eat, and hit the road. He sighed.

Nicole wriggled around and raised up onto her elbow. "Hey, Hannigan. Everything all right?" Her voice was softly teasing, warm and tantalizing.

"Sure," he said evenly, giving her a slight grin. Even that was an effort when he didn't feel at all like smiling. Their relationship was getting dangerously close to the real thing, and he was divided over it.

But he didn't want to start confessing his indecisiveness to Nicole. Regardless of his confused state of mind—definitely not her fault—she was a special woman. The problem was that he had to make up his mind about himself before he could involve someone else in his life, especially a woman whom he knew had deep and tender feelings for him.

Nicole sat up abruptly, tugging on the edge of the sheet to cover her breasts. "Know what I'd like to do now?"

For some reason he became wary. "What?"

"Talk."

"Talk about what?" He could feel himself mentally retreating from the idea.

"About you." She put on a serious expression—not altogether effective because of the twinkle in her eyes—and spoke in the somber voice of a newscaster relating an incident of tragic proportions. "The question is, folks, just who *is* Officer Tuck Hannigan, and what is it that lies under his thick layer of cop skin?"

"Cop skin?" Tuck had to laugh, and it wasn't an effort, either. "You're sort of a kook, do you know that?"

"Is that a polite word for 'crazy'?" she asked pertly.

His smile faded, and he couldn't resist touching her. Gently his fingertips caressed her cheek. "You're not crazy," he said softly.

She took a breath and still sounded breathless. "Yes, I am. Crazy about you, mister."

His fingers stopped moving, though they remained on her cheek. "Don't say that, Nicole. You don't really know me." In the next instant he left her altogether and slid off the bed. "We've got to get going."

Her eyes followed his movements while an unbearable ache grew in her midsection. He pulled on his underwear and jeans, then gathered his other things and walked to the door between their rooms. "Can you be ready in fifteen minutes?"

"I can be ready in ten," she said dully. What was there to do, other than take a quick shower?

"Okay. See you then." Walking out, he closed her side of the connecting door behind him. Listening intently, she heard another click: he had also locked his side of the door.

* * *

"How does that place look to you?" Tuck asked. They had left the motel, stopped to gas the car, and were now seeking a restaurant. At least Tuck was. Nicole's thoughts were as far from food as they could get.

"It looks fine," she said with barely a glance at the blue-and-white building. It bore a sign: Tommy's Steak House. Even though breakfast hadn't been exactly hardy and had taken place about five hours ago, the thought of a steak turned her stomach.

Tuck pulled into Tommy's parking lot and turned off the ignition. Nicole's blue mood was easily recognized and he felt guilty as hell because he'd caused it.

"Come on. A good meal will make you feel a lot better."

Her eyes snapped suddenly. "Don't be a jerk, Tuck. Thus far, that's the one thing you *haven't* been!" It wasn't completely true. Several times she'd put him in the jerk category, but she'd never said it to his face until now. She opened her door and climbed out.

They traipsed into the restaurant and were shown to a booth. The waitress laid down menus. "May I get you something to drink while you're looking over the menu?"

"Coffee," Tuck ordered.

"Do you have a bar?" Nicole asked, earning a sharp look from Tuck.

"Yes, ma'am. What would you like?"

"A vodka martini, straight up. Make it a double."

The waitress walked away and Tuck sat back with his eyes narrowed on Nicole. "So, you like vodka martinis? I never would have guessed."

"Frankly, I don't care for the taste of liquor of any kind. Other than some varieties of wine." Her expression was cold and unfriendly. "But a stiff drink might make me forget what a complete moron I've been with you."

"You haven't been a moron." With his teeth clenched, he looked away for a moment, his gaze drifting around the nearly vacant dining room. Finally he looked at Nicole again. "If either of us is a moron, it's me."

"Yeah, right," she drawled sarcastically. "I didn't hear *you* saying you were crazy about someone who apparently would rather contract leprosy than fall in love."

Tuck's expression turned hard. "I think this conversation is over." The waitress delivered Tuck's coffee and Nicole's double martini. "Thanks," he said to the woman.

Nicole picked up her drink with a rebellious expression. "You think all you have to do is say 'I think this conversation is over,' and that's the end of it. You really have an ego, don't you? Maybe that's your problem, Hannigan. Maybe you think you're so much better than anyone else, you can't bring your own self-esteem down to the level of the rest of us humans." She took a healthy swallow. "You've probably *never* been in love," she added disdainfully.

"What's so great about love?" he shot back at her. "All it does is bind two people together when they'd probably each be better off alone."

"So sayeth the wizard," she drawled in a scathing tone. "I suppose you have firsthand experience to back up that statement?"

"As a matter of fact, I do."

She waited, but he said no more. "I should have known you wouldn't talk about it. But tell me this, Hannigan. What do you do when you're through with a woman? Do you bother with goodbyes, or do you just vanish into thin air?" She laughed derogatorily and took another swallow of her martini. "Guess I'll find out, won't I?"

His eyes were dark gray and bottomless. "You don't have any reason to attack me like this. I didn't force you into anything. You got exactly what you wanted."

"Kind devil, aren't you?"

The waitress appeared with her pad and pencil. "Ready to order?"

"Yes," Tuck said before Nicole could answer. "I'll have a T-bone steak, medium rare, a baked potato and a salad with oil and vinegar dressing."

The woman looked at Nicole. "I'll have another double martini," she said grimly.

Tuck's jaw clenched. "Bring the lady a hamburger and french fries." He knew she liked burgers and fries, because she'd bought them on the trip from Vegas to Idaho. "Bring her some coffee, too, and I'd like a refill."

"Right away, sir."

Nicole smiled sweetly. "Trying to save me from myself?"

"You're drinking on an empty stomach and we're going to be on the road very soon. I'd rather you weren't sick, if you don't mind."

Her smile turned into a glare. "Maybe you'd like to return to that motel and have one more go at me before we leave."

"Dammit, Nicole, that's enough!"

"Go to hell," she muttered, and tossed back the rest of her drink.

"You're behaving like a child," he said with pronounced disgust.

"You're not," she shot back. "You're behaving like every woman's worst nightmare." She leaned forward to snap, "Do you think I fall into bed with every man who hints that I should? Didn't you know what you were doing to me, or didn't you care?"

He put his elbow on the table and his forehead into his hand, rubbing it wearily with his fingertips. "What do you want me to say? I'm sorry you got hurt. I'm sorry I ever touched you."

"Not as sorry as I am," she said bitterly. Her second drink was delivered, and she immediately picked it up for a swallow. She was beginning to feel the effects of the strong drinks. Her mind was swimming and her mouth wasn't working well. She hadn't overindulged since her college days, and it was true what she'd told Tuck about disliking hard liquor. Making a fool of herself by getting drunk seemed to somehow be a method of getting back at Tuck, which even she knew was a pretty sad commentary on her state of mind.

But she was hurt and angry and frustrated. Why had Tuck evaded conversation with her at the motel? How could he be so crass as to make unbelievably passionate love with her and then act as though she should forget it the minute it was over? She wanted to hurt him as he'd hurt her, and didn't know how to accomplish it. Deep down she knew her argumentative attitude was only making him withdraw even more, but she couldn't be nice to him, she just couldn't.

When a cup of coffee was set in front of her, she alternated sips of it with sips of the martini. Then their food was delivered, and she ate a few french fries while Tuck hungrily consumed his steak. That infuriated her, too, him sitting there eating as though everything was just great in his world.

Maybe it was, she thought with a pang of utter agony. After all, who was she but an interlude in his life, a break from his ordinary routines?

He saved your life, a voice in her head said with painful distinction. Yes, he'd saved her life, more than once, to be factual. And God knew she was grateful. But did he have to make her fall in love with him in the process?

She suddenly felt defeated and broken. Nothing she could say or do was going to make him love her. It didn't work that way. No woman could make a man fall in love with her, not by sleeping with him and certainly not by haranguing him. Shoving the unfinished martini aside, she nibbled at her hamburger.

Tuck glanced up and saw what was happening. Her defeated expression was a hundred times more effective at making him feel like a horse's rear end than her anger and cutting words could ever have been.

Thoughtfully he finished his meal. Nicole didn't deserve the silent treatment from him. He felt a great deal for her. Maybe it was love, maybe it wasn't. He shouldn't be so reticent with her. A little conversation wouldn't kill him.

But not here, not in a public place. He would do his talking in the car.

He laid his napkin on the table. "Let me know when you're through eating," he said, simply because her disinterest in the food on her plate was so obvious.

Nicole pushed her plate away. "I'm through now."

"Would you like anything else? Some dessert?"

"No, I'm finished."

"Then we'll leave." Picking up the check, Tuck got out of the booth and walked over to the cash register.

Nicole slid from the booth and headed for the ladies' room. Washing her hands, she noticed their tremor. Her head was dizzy from those drinks and she felt like an idiot. Tuck had been right to call her behavior childish; she had never in her life done anything so outlandish.

Sighing, she dried her hands on a paper towel. It wasn't going to be easy, but she had to stop thinking of Tuck in her future. It wasn't going to happen, and the sooner she faced and accepted that fact, the better off she would be.

Time suddenly entered her mind. They had left Vegas . . . when? And what was today? How long had they been together? Long enough for her to truly fall in love, or was she merely infatuated with Hannigan's tough and sexy exterior?

Whatever, she had made enough of a fool out of herself for one day. Tuck would hear no more snide remarks from her, nor any questions. She did have *some* pride left, after all.

They were at least twenty miles into their trip south when Tuck said out of the blue, "Nicole, I was married once."

Startled, her head came around slowly to see him. He was looking straight ahead, as though the road would vanish if he didn't stare at it. She honestly didn't know what to say, though the questions she had promised herself not to ask him anymore were again stacking up in her mind.

"I had a son," he said quietly. "He died of pneumonia when he was only a few months old."

"Oh, my God," she whispered, closing her eyes at the onslaught of pain she felt for what he must have suffered.

"I was divorced shortly after," he said.

She couldn't stay silent any longer. "How long were you married?"

"Three years. It wasn't a good marriage from the start, and after Timmy's death there just didn't seem to be any point to keep on trying."

"Why wasn't it a good marriage? You must have loved her to marry her."

"I did, but it didn't last. Nicole, there's something you have to understand. The divorce rate among police officers is very high. Most cops work crazy hours. Wives never know for sure when their husbands will be home. Countless dinners are either warmed up or thrown out. Children wait for their fathers to come home and, with conflicting schedules, sometimes don't see them for days. Some wives can't live with the worry. Their men face danger day after day, and it preys on their minds. I've seen it happen again and again. Cops like being cops, and a lot of wives can't understand that and end up hating their husbands' career. The breach gets wider and wider until there's no way to bridge it."

"Is that what happened with you and your wife?"

"It was part of it." He didn't want to bring up Jeanie's running around and leaving their ill infant son with a neighborhood teenager. "There were other things, but that was part of it," he repeated.

"Are you saying there are no good marriages in the department?"

Tuck sent her a startled look. "No. Some of the guys I work with have very solid marriages. But their wives are different, Nicole. They don't spend every waking moment worrying about their husbands getting killed by some dope head. I know one couple in particular that I have a great deal of admiration for. Kelly—that's the wife—told me that when they were first married, she never slept a night through when Ray was on night duty. But then one day she realized that she was making herself—and Ray—miserable. She's an intelligent woman and made the decision then and there to *stop* worrying."

"She must be very strong."

"She is, but she's a rare case, Nicole. Too many wives simply can't deal with the stress."

"Why are you telling me this?"

"You said you wanted me to talk about myself."

"Yes, but after..." She drew a breath. "Well, I never expected you to do it. I'm terribly sorry about your son. I can't imagine anything worse than losing a child."

"It's been more than ten years now," he said, indicating that time had diminished his grief.

He looked tired, Nicole realized. Instead of resting, they had made love. Not just today, but last night, as well. If that was the end of it for him, why had he decided to tell her about himself?

"You confuse me," she said with a despondent sigh. Her head was aching, a result of that silly impulse to drink lunch instead of eating it.

"Probably," Tuck agreed. Why wouldn't she be confused? Rattled was an even better word. She'd been forced to leave her home and to accept him as her protector and companion. Then, instead of maintaining a sensible distance between them, he'd made pass after pass. Being the kind of woman she was, she had construed his attentions and her own response as love.

Well, maybe it *was* love, but he wasn't sure he wanted to be in love. His own personal problems weren't completely settled in his mind, though without question he'd proved himself at the lake cabin. He was still a cop and a damned good one. His instincts were as keen as they'd ever been.

There was only one thing about the events at the cabin that kept him uneasy: he hadn't pulled the trigger on that thug with the bomb. Would he have done so before the convenience store killings?

Nicole was still thinking about confusion. "Are you feeling confused, too?" she asked.

"About us?"

"Yes, about us."

He shot her a glance, then heaved a sigh. "More than you could possibly know."

Tuck took Highway 93 south and they drove into Jackpot, Nevada, around seven that evening. To Nicole's surprise, he pulled into the parking lot of a large hotel-casino.

"We'll stay here tonight," he announced, turning off the ignition.

"I thought we'd be driving straight through. Won't Captain Crawford be expecting us?"

"I told him on the phone not to expect us until sometime tomorrow. We'll get a good night's sleep and start the last leg of the trip in the morning. We'll be in Vegas before tomorrow night."

Nicole let him make all the decisions without offering any suggestions. He rented two rooms, again side-by-side. They brought their things in and then went to one of the casino's restaurants for dinner. This time Nicole ate—she ordered Chinese food, which turned out to be exceptionally good—instead of playing childish games with martinis. It was only about nine when they walked back to their rooms and said good-night in the corridor. Tuck went into his room and Nicole into hers. She was positive he wouldn't knock on the connecting door tonight, and he didn't. She showered, got into her pajamas and went to bed.

It was then, while she was lying there awaiting sleep, that she recognized Tuck's earlier conversation for what it was: his way of discouraging her interest in him. Maybe because her brain had been a little woozy from her liquid lunch, she hadn't grasped his motive for suddenly sharing part of himself with her. *The divorce rate is high among cops. Most wives can't live with the stress.*

Nicole angrily punched her pillow. She was too damned gullible to be believed. That had been her opening to bring the generalities he was spouting down to one specific cop— him. Instead, she had gotten soppy-eyed over the death of his infant son and then let Hannigan ramble on about how tough it was for cops to maintain relationships. The one intelligent question she'd asked—weren't there any stable marriages in the department?—he had stumbled over his own tongue in describing how different the wives were in those successful liaisons. Which was a slap in the face, wasn't it? Indicating that *she* was much too emotional, or some damned thing, to ever be a cop's wife.

He *was* a jerk. Worse, he was a sexual opportunist, taking advantage of her fear and of his role as a big, strong protector. Of course she had turned to him. He'd probably known in advance that would happen.

Well, he needn't worry about her bothering him once she was on her own turf again. Even if they should run into each other accidentally, which wasn't very likely, her reaction would be as cool and distant as she could make it.

In the darkness of her room, tears gathered in her eyes and she angrily brushed them away. She had lived without Tuck Hannigan in her life for a good many years and she certainly could do so again. To hell with him. He was nothing but a heartbreaker. Who needed it?

Tuck had showered and gotten into bed, but as exhausted as his body was, his mind wouldn't shut down.

Did he love Nicole or had he made love to her because she was sexy, beautiful and handy? He wasn't comfortable with that idea, but it was a possibility.

If that were the case, what did it make him? Not that he hadn't taken women to bed without feeling guilty about it afterward. But those women had known the score before-hand. Nicole was not a one-night-stander, even if *he* was.

His lips thinned. Was that what his life had come down to, a series of one-night stands? True, they'd been few and far between, but not since his marriage had he permitted himself to feel anything for a woman.

This was not a subject he'd given any thought to before tonight, and he didn't like it, probably because it smacked of some discomfiting truths about himself. He was not a happy man, nor could he remember when happiness had been more than a word to him. His thoughts became con-fused and disoriented as bits and pieces of his life flashed through his mind. He could feel himself sinking deeper into a morass of depression and loneliness.

Finally one clear thought seeped into his brain: he had to talk to someone, a professional. Dr. Laura Keaton would do. He would contact her office for an appointment when he got home.

Thirteen

Wearing her last pair of clean jeans and a simple white blouse, Nicole slid into the booth in the hotel-casino's coffee shop. Tuck was already there, drinking coffee and waiting to order breakfast until she arrived. She had called his room and asked him to meet her there. "There's something I have to do, but I won't be long, maybe fifteen, twenty minutes."

He'd agreed. She didn't need his company for reasons of safety now, but he did wonder what her errand or task was.

As soon as they had ordered breakfast, she told him about it, coolly and while looking directly into his eyes across the table. "I'm flying home from here. I chartered a small plane. I'm using the cash given to me the night we left Vegas, along with my own credit card, to pay for the flight. I'll be leaving in—" she checked her watch "—forty-five minutes."

Her expression said clearly, *Are you going to try to stop me?*

His stomach turned over. If that determined glint in her eyes was any measure, there was only one way to stop her, and he couldn't use physical force on Nicole.

"Well," he said tonelessly, "you're a free agent. Do whatever you want."

"I intend to," she said coldly.

Breakfast was delivered and they ate it in stony silence. Tuck picked up the check. "Do you have your suitcase stashed somewhere, or is it still in your room?"

They got to their feet. "It's in my room."

"Wait while I pay, and I'll walk with you."

"Why?"

"You have enough time. Just wait," he demanded sharply, speaking through clenched teeth. During their silent breakfast his system had gone haywire, mixing disappointment with anger, self-reproach with resentment of Nicole's attitude. He had wanted today with her, hours together in the car. Maybe by the time they had reached Vegas, they would have been on better terms. She had neatly destroyed his last opportunity to let her know...

Let her know what? That he had deeply rooted feelings for her and just didn't know how to express them?

After paying the check, they trudged through the casino to the hotel lobby and then down the long corridor that led to their rooms.

It was only when Nicole was fitting her key into the lock on her door that Tuck finally spoke. "I'll be calling Joe Crawford to let him know you'll be flying in."

She pushed the door open and turned to face him. "I don't think that's necessary."

His expression darkened. "How in hell would you know what is or isn't necessary?"

Her eyes blazed with sudden fury. "I've had about all of your overbearing, better-than-thou tactics I can take. Just because I'm not a cop doesn't mean I don't have a brain. Suppose you get off your high horse for two minutes and *explain* why calling Captain Crawford is necessary."

"Because he's expecting you to arrive with me!"

"Don't you dare shout at me! There are people around, you . . . you cretin!"

Tuck looked up and down the corridor and saw not one single person. With his jaw clenched, he moved quickly and pushed Nicole through the open door of her room. Before she could do more than gasp, he had turned her around, shut the door and shoved her up against it, pressing her into it with the weight of his own body.

His eyes glittered dangerously. His hands held hers above her head. His chest all but flattened her breasts. "Are we going to resort to name-calling now?"

"Why are you doing this? I have to go," she said with a frantic edge to her voice. "You know I have to go." There was a hotel car waiting to take her to Jackpot's airstrip.

But the panic she felt wasn't because of that waiting car. She could deny her feelings for this man till doomsday, but all Tuck had to do to make her want him was something like this, touch her, push himself against her, hold his head so that his mouth was but a fraction from hers. He hadn't manhandled her like this before, and God knew she didn't approve of caveman tactics, but his hard body pressing into hers was exciting and unmercifully arousing.

He moved his hips, hunching them forward. "See what you do to me?" he whispered thickly.

She couldn't *see* what she did to him, not in their present positions, but she could certainly feel it. If he kissed her she'd forget about that plane, she thought weakly, and she didn't want to spend another long day in the car with him.

She took a breath and forced herself to speak without emotion or even a hint of friendliness. "Take your hands off of me this minute. I've had it with you, Tuck. I want no more of you. Is that plain enough?"

He stiffened. "Do you really mean that?"

"I mean it with every fiber of my being."

The pain that ricocheted throughout his system wasn't a pleasant sensation, but pride kept his chin up.

Releasing her, he stepped back. Nicole ducked around him and went for her suitcase, which was all set to go. She picked it up. Her pulse was running wild with soft, female emotions, but she managed to lay a hard and fierce look on Tuck.

"Do I have to fight you to get out of here?" she asked.

"No." He opened the door for her. "See you in Vegas," he said grimly.

She brushed past him. "Don't count on it."

It didn't surprise Nicole to see detectives John Harper and Scott Paulsen waiting for her when she deplaned in Las Vegas.

After a cursory greeting, John said, "We're going to escort you to the prosecutor's office. He's anxious to talk to you."

She sighed to herself, thinking, *And so it begins.*

Dr. Laura Keaton greeted Tuck with a handshake and an invitation to sit down.

They both sat, in the very same chairs they had used in every one of Tuck's previous sessions with the psychologist.

Laura smiled. "How have you been?"

Tuck *didn't* smile. "Not very damned good."

"Tell me about it."

Thirty minutes later she knew it all, everything that had occurred since their last meeting, down to the smallest detail. Laura had listened with very few comments, thinking all the while that this was a different man than she had counseled before.

When Tuck had wound down, she asked quietly, "What do you want me to say, Tuck? What do you want to hear?"

He laughed, sharply, bitterly. "Maybe that I'm not crazy."

"That's an easy one. You're not crazy. Does hearing me say that make you feel any better?"

"No." He'd been looking at his boots. His eyes lifted. "What am I afraid of, Doc?"

"Not of police work, obviously. From what you've told me, you handled things very well in Coeur d'Alene."

"Except for not shooting that piece of slime when I had him in the sights of my gun."

"You were thinking of Nicole. Protecting her was your primary goal, which you accomplished. You should be feeling very proud of yourself, not questioning your reactions."

"What if it happens again? What if I'm in a situation where I *should* use my gun and I can't do it?"

"My professional opinion is that you will use it if a situation calls for gunfire. Tuck, you did the right thing in Coeur d'Alene. How can you doubt it, when you saved Miss Currie's life at great risk to your own?"

Laura's expression softened. "Let's talk a little more about Nicole. That's where your fear really lies, Tuck."

He drew in a slow, discomfited breath. "Yeah, I know."

"Don't be afraid of love, Tuck. Thank your lucky stars that you met a woman you *can* love. And don't look for guarantees. There are none, not in any human relationship. We all have so many flaws that it's a wonder men and women ever get together. Or stay together. But they do, Tuck, they do. What you have to ask yourself, and only you can answer, is if you love this woman enough to try and work through the adjustments that are absolutely necessary for any couple to make it."

Laura paused. "Does she love you?"

"I...don't know."

Glancing at her watch, Laura got to her feet. "Then that's your first order of business, isn't it? Finding out how Nicole feels about you? I'm sorry, but I have another appointment, Tuck. Will you come back and talk to me again, say in about a week?"

Tuck nodded. "I'll make an appointment on my way out. Thanks, Doc."

She smiled. "Good luck, Officer Hannigan."

Nicole went back to work and was welcomed with bright smiles from her assistants, and a meeting with two of the vice presidents of the Monte Carlo. They assured her that however long the trial of Nick Lowicki might take, her job was secure.

In turn, she passed on her own assurances. "The prosecutor told me that my testimony shouldn't take more than a couple of days. Maybe not even that long. It depends on the defense attorney's cross-examination."

After work, for several days, she went shopping. She'd left most of her business suits hanging in her closet while packing for her forced trip, thank goodness, but she was pitifully short of blouses and underwear. Four suitcases had been stuffed full, after all, and other than the few pairs of jeans and tops she'd returned home with, all of her casual clothing—shorts, slacks, T-shirts, jackets and shoes—had been destroyed in the fire. There'd been lots of lingerie lost, as well, lovely things, lovely *expensive* things. Some dresses, both informal and dressy, including accessories, were on her list for reimbursement, though she'd gone light in that department, thinking, correctly, while doing her initial packing, that there probably wouldn't be very many occasions to dress up.

But the list she'd given Detective Harper had been very long, filling several sheets of paper. There'd been costume jewelry on it, some of it quite costly, and several purses and scarves, a lot of little things that she wondered now why on earth she'd taken with her. As distraught as she'd been at the time, however, it was a small miracle that she hadn't taken every piece of clothing she'd owned.

She was determined to forget Tuck and during working hours managed fairly well to stick with that attitude. But the evenings played dirty tricks with her mind. Shopping herself into exhaustion didn't help all that much, because once the stores closed for the day, she had to go home. Of course, she was completely aware of the unmarked police car parked out front every night, but whatever officers were on duty never came to the house. They were unknown entities, cops without faces to her, and as long as one of them wasn't Tuck, she was able to ignore their presence, though she felt their diligence wasn't necessary. Lowicki was locked up and Gil Spencer was dead. According to the prosecutor, their organization was not only in shambles, Lowicki's cohorts wanted nothing to do with a murder charge and were singing like canaries.

Of course, that progression of thoughts never failed to remind her of Tuck's caustic question. *How would you know what is or isn't necessary?* Then she would remember his body pressing hers against the door of her room, and another scar would appear on her already badly damaged heart.

She contacted all of her friends and called her mother. Her life was getting back to normal, even if she wasn't. The truth was that she would never again be the same trusting, somewhat naive woman she'd once been. Too much had changed, not only because of the witness protection program but because of Tuck.

The night was a hundred degrees and moonless, dark as a well. Tuck's palms were sweating, his mouth was dry and his heart was pounding. It didn't matter; this was something he had to do.

Spotting the unmarked police car as he stopped his own car at the curb, he switched off his headlights, got out and walked over to the officers to identify himself.

The vehicle's windows were all open, though there was no breeze to catch. Even if there had been, they would have been hot. "Hey, Hannigan. How's it going?"

"Doubletree and—" Tuck peered into the vehicle "—Parsons. Having fun out here, boys?"

"Yeah, right. Stakeout's your favorite duty, too, isn't it?" Doubletree said sarcastically. "What're you doing here, Hannigan?"

"Paying Miss Currie a visit."

The two men in the car snickered. "Official business, of course."

"What else?" Tuck said smoothly. Although he still hadn't returned to work and thus had had little contact with his co-workers, it was obvious from Doubtletree's and Parson's snicker that word had gotten around about him being the cop who'd taken Nicole to Idaho for witness protection.

Tuck straightened and slapped the top of the car. "Try to stay cool, boys. See you later." He started to walk away.

"Hey, Tuck. Ask the lady if she's got a couple of cold sodas for two thirsty cops."

"I'll ask." Tuck started up Nicole's front walk, noting the lighted windows in her house and the exterior lamp lighting the small court only steps from the door. His heart started hammering again. She might slam the door in his face. She might tell him to get the hell out of her sight. An urge to forget the whole thing, to just turn around and return to his car, was tough to combat.

He forced himself to continue to her door and to ring the doorbell.

Nicole was in her bedroom. She'd gone shopping again after work and there were parcels of clothing still to be hung in her closet. But she'd been hot and tired when she'd gotten home, and had decided to take a shower before putting away her new things.

She was wearing a cool, cotton robe, knee-length, and just starting on the packages when the doorbell rang. Frowning, she glanced at the clock on the bedstand. It wasn't that late, not quite ten, but her friends didn't drop in unannounced at this hour. The cops in the unmarked car had never come near the house before, but it could be one of them, she thought, laying down the package and leaving her bedroom.

At the front door she peered through the tiny peephole. Her heart nearly stopped when she saw Tuck's face. Breathless and slightly panicky, she backed away from the door. Why was he here? What did he want from her now?

The doorbell pealed again. Gathering her wits about her and tightening the sash of her robe, she composed her features and opened the door.

"Hello," he said quietly, belying the nervousness running rampant in his system.

She nodded. "Hello."

"May I come in?"

"Uh..." She honestly didn't know what to do. If she let him in, what then? But if she said no, wouldn't she forever wonder why he had come?

Stepping back, she held the door open in invitation. "Come in."

"Thanks." Relief of enormous magnitude diminished some of Tuck's tension.

She brought him to the living room. "Sit down, if you'd like."

They both sat. Nicole couldn't believe how fit he looked. He was wearing jeans and a white T-shirt, and he was so handsome he took her breath. His skin was deeply tanned and he actually looked relaxed.

In fact, his insides were so tight, he wondered if they would ever unwind.

"What've you been doing, lying in the sun?" she asked, a little coolly, a little disdainfully.

"I've been in the sun," he admitted. "What I did was rent a houseboat out at the lake. I needed to do some thinking." When she made no response, he added, "About us."

"Us?" Her left eyebrow shot up. But deep inside of her a thrill had come to life. She'd told herself a hundred times that falling for Tuck Hannigan and then letting him know about it was the most stupid thing she had ever done. Except for making love with him, that is. All of her self-help recriminations meant beans, apparently, when all he had to do was show up looking like a dream and mention that he'd been thinking of "us" for her insides to turn to jelly.

"I didn't know there was an 'us,' " she said with some haughtiness, an effort to protect herself from further involvement with a man who didn't know the meaning of the word.

"I think there is. What do you think?" Her pink-and-white robe was interesting. She looked fresh from a shower, with no makeup on her face and her hair damp. He'd be willing to bet that robe was all there was. No underwear, no nightie. *Very* interesting. And exciting. He took a calming breath.

Her eyes narrowed slightly. She didn't trust him, but worse, she didn't trust herself. "What brought this on?"

"I just told you. I've been thinking about us." He leaned forward, laying his forearms on his thighs. "Nicole, I love you."

She nearly fainted. "You *what?*"

He got up to pace back and forth in front of her, which she didn't need. Already her nerves were in shambles, and watching his long, lean body in movement was giving her hot flashes.

He seemed agitated. "I know this is a shock for you, but it's a shock for me, too. I've been going in circles since..." He stopped to frown. "Damn, those circles started the night we met." He began pacing again. "But a person can't be afraid of love. I finally got that through my thick skull."

"You...were...afraid of...love?" she whispered, too weak and shaken to even speak normally. He loved her? Was it possible?

He suddenly knelt in front of her. There was a piercing, almost feverish glitter in his eyes. "We don't choose who we fall in love with. We don't choose *to* fall in love. It's something that happens without consent or intent."

She was nearly speechless, mesmerized by his eyes and what he was saying. "Tuck..." It had a helpless sound.

"You said you were crazy about me. Do you remember?" Her head bobbed once. "Nicole, I have to ask. Do you love me?"

She swallowed. "If I said yes, what...what would you do?"

"Propose."

"But you said marriages in the department don't usually work out."

"I said a lot of fool things. Nicole, I've gone around and around on this. Whoever said everyone falls in love with the perfect person? Maybe love hurts anyone dumb enough to... to do it. It does hurt, I know. It's made me suffer and question my own sanity.

"Maybe we'd argue. Hell, I know we wouldn't agree on every little thing. Maybe you'd worry about me, and maybe I'd worry about you. But, honey, I have this great big hole right here..." He placed his hand on his chest. "And you're the only thing in the whole damned world that can fill it."

She was sitting so still, as though frozen in place, and staring at him.

"You're really shook, aren't you?" he asked softly.

"Yes," she whispered.

"Maybe there's something we can do about that." His hands crept up her robe to clasp her waist, and he leaned forward to press his lips to hers. It was a gentle, tender kiss that melted the last remnants of ice in her system. "Tell me you love me," he whispered.

She sucked in a long breath. "I...love you."

"Oh, baby," he groaned, and began undoing the sash of her robe. Pushing aside its panels, he buried his face in her bare breasts.

She held his head and felt tears stinging her eyes and nose. They dripped down her cheeks and onto his hair. She laughed, shakily. "I'm getting your hair wet."

He raised his head to see her teary eyes. "Why are you crying?"

"Because I'm so happy."

A smile broke out on his face. "Me, too." Getting to his feet, he pulled her from the chair and lifted her off the floor and up into his arms. Then he remembered something. "Have you got a couple of cold sodas in your refrigerator?"

"What?"

He laughed. "I promised the cops outside I'd bring them some sodas, if you had any."

"There's a variety in the refrigerator. Help yourself."

He set her on her feet. "Don't go away."

While he raced to the kitchen and then outside, Nicole went to her bedroom. She tossed the robe and got into bed. She was in love with a cop and things wouldn't always be as rosy as they felt right now.

But she had never been happier and would take the bad with the good. She smiled and listened for Tuck's return.

Epilogue

"And so I told her everything I'd been feeling and going through," Tuck said. "Including my sessions with you."

Laura Keaton nodded. "Wise decision, Tuck."

Tuck grinned. "Can I put your name on our guest list? The wedding's set for September 8."

"By all means." He was in uniform. "I see you've gone back to work."

"Started on Monday."

"And how is it out there?"

"Same old, same old, Doc. Nothing changes on the street. Lock up one drug pusher and two more spring up."

"Tell me this, Tuck. How is Nicole dealing with having to testify at Lowicki's trial? Incidentally, when does it start?"

"It starts in another week, and she's dealing with it like a little trooper. She's some special woman, Laura."

Laura smiled. "Maybe the love between you makes her special. And vice versa."

"I'm not special, Doc."

"No?" Laura laughed softly. "I'll bet if you said that to Nicole you'd get an argument."

He thought about the passion and love between him and Nicole, then nodded. "Yeah, you're right. I'd get a hell of an argument."

Glancing at his watch, he rose from his chair. "Gotta go." He took a step toward Dr. Keaton and offered his hand, which she gladly took. "Thanks for everything, Doc. You're the best."

At the door he turned. "By the way, I don't smoke anymore. Just thought you'd like to know." He went out whistling.

Dr. Keaton sat there for a moment with a satisfied expression, then got up and went to her desk. She pressed the intercom button. "I'm ready for my next appointment, Clarisse."

* * * * *

SILHOUETTE® Desire®

COMING NEXT MONTH

Take 4 bestselling love stories FREE

Plus get a FREE surprise gift!

As seen on TV!
Free Gift Offer

With a Free Gift proof-of-purchase from any Silhouette® book,
you can receive a beautiful cubic zirconia pendant.

This gorgeous marquise-shaped stone is a genuine cubic
zirconia—accented by an 18" gold tone necklace.

(Approximate retail value $19.95)

Send for yours today...
compliments of ▼ *Silhouette*®
™

To receive your free gift, a cubic zirconia pendant, send us one original proof-of-
purchase, photocopies not accepted, from the back of any Silhouette Romance™,
Silhouette Desire®, Silhouette Special Edition®, Silhouette Intimate Moments®
or Silhouette Shadows™ title available in February, March or April at your favorite
retail outlet, together with the Free Gift Certificate, plus a check or money order for
$1.75 U.S./$2.25 CAN. (do not send cash) to cover postage and handling, payable
to Silhouette Free Gift Offer. We will send you the specified gift. Allow 6 to 8 weeks for
delivery. Offer good until April 30, 1996 or while quantities last. Offer valid in the U.S. and
Canada only.

Free Gift Certificate

Name: _____

Address: _____

City: _____ State/Province: _____ Zip/Postal Code: _____

Mail this certificate, one proof-of-purchase and a check or money order for postage
and handling to: SILHOUETTE FREE GIFT OFFER 1996. In the U.S.: 3010 Walden
Avenue, P.O. Box 9057, Buffalo NY 14269-9057. In Canada: P.O. Box 622, Fort Erie,

---

FREE GIFT OFFER   079-KBZ-R
ONE PROOF-OF-PURCHASE
To collect your fabulous FREE GIFT, a cubic zirconia pendant, you must include this
original proof-of-purchase for each gift with the properly completed Free Gift Certificate.

079-KBZ-R

Are your lips succulent, impetuous, delicious or racy?

Find out in a very special Valentine's Day promotion—THAT SPECIAL KISS!

Inside four special Harlequin and Silhouette February books are details for THAT SPECIAL KISS! explaining how you can have your lip prints read by a romance expert.

Look for details in the following series books, written by four of Harlequin and Silhouette readers' favorite authors:

Silhouette Intimate Moments #691
Mackenzie's Pleasure by *New York Times* bestselling author Linda Howard

Harlequin Romance #3395
Because of the Baby by Debbie Macomber

Silhouette Desire #979
Megan's Marriage by Annette Broadrick

Harlequin Presents #1793
The One and Only by Carole Mortimer

Fun, romance, four top-selling authors, plus a FREE gift! This is a very special Valentine's Day you won't want to miss! Only from Harlequin and Silhouette.

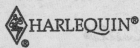 

VAL96

You're About to Become a

Privileged Woman

Reap the rewards of fabulous free gifts and benefits with proofs-of-purchase from Silhouette and Harlequin books

Pages & Privileges™

It's our way of thanking you for buying our books at your favorite retail stores.

Harlequin and Silhouette—
the most privileged readers in the world!

For more information about Harlequin and Silhouette's PAGES & PRIVILEGES program call the Pages & Privileges Benefits Desk: 1-503-794-2499

SD-PP107